S0-COP-890

DATE DUE

THE THROBBING DARK

It wasn't what you could call a quiet night. The Fijian drums were beating out the rhythms of the natives' full-throated chants, Australians from the sugar mill were celebrating a bumper win in the Tasmanian sweepstake with drinking songs — to the accompaniment of steel guitar, ukulele and a fist fight — and Jack How's gramophone was enlivening the drinking party in his firm's batchelor quarters. Throughout the night the drums continued to throb — but in the morning How was dead in his bed. Everything pointed to his bitter enemy Joe Boreman — except that Boreman, too, had been murdered.

FRANK ARTHUR

THE THROBBING DARK

Complete and Unabridged

LINFORD
Leicester

First published in Great Britain in 1963 by
Herbert Jenkins Limited
London

First Linford Edition
published November 1990

British Library CIP Data

Arthur, Frank, *1902–1984*
    The throbbing dark. — Large print ed. —
Linford mystery library
I. Title
823.912[F]

ISBN 0–7089–6993–3

Published by
F. A. Thorpe (Publishing) Ltd.
Anstey, Leicestershire

Set by Words & Graphics Ltd.
Anstey, Leicestershire
Printed and bound in Great Britain by
T. J. Press (Padstow) Ltd., Padstow, Cornwall

Dedication to:

H. E. SNELL

who sent me to the West Coast, and
brought me back to Suva; this slight
return for much kindness.

Author's Note

This story is a work of fiction, and all the people in it are fictitious. The action takes place in Malua, an entirely imaginary place in the Fiji Islands. I do not intend that any of the characters should be taken to be the portraits of people who live, or who have lived, in Fiji or the South Seas; and I have tried to make the characters unlike anyone I knew in Fiji. I have done my best not to use the names of people who were there in my time or who may have come there since. Spearpoint apart, the names have been taken from a list of people who were living in England over two hundred years ago; and if there are people alive and associated with Fiji bearing the same names, I can assure them that I am not aware of their existence.

Frank Arthur.

Prologue

INSPECTOR SPEARPOINT, of the
Fiji Constabulary, posted to the Malua
District after his stint at Suva, had
barely settled down on the West Coast
before he was confronted with a problem
which began like this:

They had never liked each other; and
when they had been baching together
for four months without companions to
absorb the tension, they came to blows.

Jack How, dressing before breakfast,
was chirruping *Bye-bye, Blackbird* in his
reedy tenor.

Boreman shouted from his room at
the other end of the veranda, "Cut out
that bloody row!"

The tune faltered, and then continued,
louder.

"I said: shut up!"

"Black-bird! Bye! Bye!"

Then, almost without pause for breath,

1

the irritating voice began on:

"I wonder if I keep on praying,
                    Char-maine! Char — "

How broke off as footsteps pounded along the veranda, and he turned to confront his messmate in the doorway.

"I told you to cut it out!"

"You don't like my singing?"

"I bloody well don't!"

"Then you'll have to lump it, won't you?"

"You'll bloody soon see if I will!"

"Char-maine!"

Boreman was six foot two and fourteen stone. He aimed a blow at where the defiance had come from, so fierce a blow that as it hit nothing it pulled him off balance.

How side-stepped and rushed in, giving the big fellow the old one-two full in the bread-basket with all his ten stone eight.

Boreman, winded, tottered backwards, floundering for balance, flinging out his arms for something to hang on to. He crashed against the veranda rail, fell twisting down the steps, collapsed on the ground, crashing his head on a fallen coconut and then rolled over, gasping.

How advanced leisurely to the rail, adjusting his bow tie, and gazed down at the fallen foe.

"Naughty temper!" he cooed. "Language! Would it calm your spirits if I were to sing you a lullaby?"

Boreman did not reply. The words he uttered were for his own comfort rather than a contribution to discussion. He was injured in several places, but he did not at once know how many or how seriously. He didn't think his back was broken, but his collision with the rail had been equivalent to a fierce kidney punch, and his cheek-bone had smashed down on a sharp stone.

When he clambered to his feet he found that he had twisted his ankle.

How's expression changed to one of concern; but his "All right?" was not so much solicitude for his foe's welfare as concern for his own responsibility if the damage proved to be serious.

Boreman merely grunted as he hobbled past. It took him so long to examine and tend his injuries that by the time he reached the breakfast table How had departed, singing blithely, to the store.

At lunch, by unspoken agreement, they began the practice which lasted almost for the rest of their lives, of sharing meals without exchanging a word or a glance.

Three nights later, when Boreman could walk more or less evenly, and the swelling under his eye had retreated so that he could see out of it, he invaded How's room, yanked aside his mosquito-net, and thrashed him with a slipper until he felt that honour was satisfied.

How felt that honour was more than satisfied. He continued to sing in the mornings, but not for so long or so loudly. Boreman, in the bar of the *Don Bradman Hotel,* muttered threats which he knew would be reported to the destined victim, but he did not live long enough to carry them out.

When young Anderton arrived to fill

the long-vacant post of assistant to the chief clerk he found that the timber-yard foreman and the motor mechanic had not spoken a word to each other for seven weeks. Nor did they welcome the intrusion into their feud of a third party. They both resented his attempts to introduce at least an outward show of cordiality into bach life.

Harry Anderton stuck it for five weeks; and then —

1

Harry Anderton's Story

ANDERTON mumbled, white-faced, "This was how I found them, Inspector. I haven't touched a thing."

"You didn't feel them — just to make sure?"

The young man shuddered. "No — no, I couldn't! I couldn't bear to stay in there. I just came out and waited for the cookboy, and then sent him for you."

"You slept through whatever happened last night, and knew nothing about it until you got up this morning?"

"Oh, no. I didn't sleep here last night. Jack How was having a rowdy party, so I cleared out and slept at the hotel. I came back for breakfast."

"Have you told the other people in the compound?" Spearpoint gestured towards the bungalows nearer the sea where the married employees of the firm lived.

"I've told no one. All I could think of was to send for you. It's all too horrible!"

Spearpoint thought: too frightened of dead men to go to his own room and change from the rumpled shirt and trousers he wore yesterday.

The bach — bachelor quarters for the staff of Richmond, Lennox & Co. consisted of five parallel rooms opening on to a front veranda, with kitchen and bathroom at the back. How, on the extreme left, and Boreman, on the extreme right, slept as far apart as possible. Anderton's room was next to How's, the centre room was the mess, and the other was unoccupied. None of the rooms had doors. The doorways had originally been fitted with hinged screens, but generations of excited bachelors had kicked holes in the netting, and the frames were now kept hooked back out of the way.

Like all European houses in Fiji, the

bungalow was built of wood, with a corrugated iron roof; and it was raised on concrete piles a couple of feet above the ground. There were two sets of steps up to the veranda: one outside How's room, which Boreman had fallen down; and one in the middle, opposite the mess room.

If Anderton was telling the truth, this was how he had found things:

Jack How's room indicated a morning after a bachelor Saturday night: empty beer-bottles, tumblers with dregs in them, cigarette butts stamped flat on the floor, the portable gramophone open with loose records piled alongside, an abandoned game on the dart-board, a pile of Australian newspapers overturned and kicked around.

How's shirt, tie, socks and trousers had been flung, with rather bad aim, at a chair. On a trunk in the far corner, a neatly-folded travelling rug looked incongruous. There was nothing to arouse Spearpoint's immediate interest — except what lay on the bed.

The bed was against the wall beside

the wide-open window. The mosquito-net was in its daytime position at the head-rail. Jack How lay flat on his back with his arms at his sides, and the upper sheet drawn neatly up to his bare shoulders. Even in August, Fiji nights are hot, and there was nothing significant in How's going to bed without a pyjama jacket.

How's face was red, his eyes and mouth open, his tongue black and protruding; and ants swarmed all over him. The tropic sun was already claiming the corpse.

Spearpoint made a visual examination, and then turned to Anderton, irresolute but fascinated in the doorway. "You're right. He's been dead for hours. No need to touch him to verify that."

Anderton's averted gaze had fixed on the rug.

"Anything particular about that rug?"

"Well — I suppose that was what he was suffocated with. The pillow is under his head. So what else could it have been? Queer! Quite right, in a way, that rug should have been used to kill him."

"What do you mean?"

"He used to boast about that rug. He used to say he'd — had more girls on that rug than — well, a great many. He used to say, 'If that ruddy rug could talk!' And now it has spoken! It's stopped his dirty tongue for ever!" The young man laughed hysterically.

"How d'you know he was suffocated?"

Anderton was taken aback. "I — I don't know. It just looks as if he was, doesn't it?"

"I'll wait for Dr. Fell's verdict. Did he usually sleep without the mosquito-net?"

"I don't think so. Perhaps he was too drunk to bother about it. When he'd been drinking a lot he used to fall asleep quite quickly. One minute he'd be singing some ribald song, and the next he'd be snoring."

"Let's see the other one."

Joe Boreman's room was tidy, but the bed and the corpse on it were not. Boreman had been shot through the head at close range. He had apparently died instantly and several hours ago. There was not much blood, but the face bore a malevolent grin and the limbs were contorted.

The chest-of-drawers a couple of feet from the bed had one drawer slightly open. On the floor under this lay an army revolver; a cord tied to the trigger led upwards and disappeared under the pillow. The mosquito-net was tucked in at the ends but hung loose at the sides; it was torn where the bullet had passed through, and on the chest-of-drawers side it was slightly smeared with blood. The reason for this was not evident.

Anderton, who again had not ventured beyond the doorway, exclaimed in excitement, "Why, look! It was a booby-trap! The gun was jammed in the drawer and tied to something under the pillow, and when he put his head on the pillow, it went off; and the force of the explosion shook the gun on to the floor, and it slid under the bed."

"Wouldn't he have seen it when he undressed?"

"If he came home late he might have gone to bed without turning on the light. But it doesn't look as if he did undress, does it?"

Boreman's right foot had been drawn up, and the knee raised, so that the sheet was rumpled back, revealing that he was wearing a grubby day-shirt.

"He took his trousers off." The trousers were lying, still belted, on a chair.

Spearpoint squeezed his bulky figure into the space between the chest-of-drawers and the bed, and crouched so that his eye was on a level with the top of the open drawer. Looking towards the pierced skull, he concluded that the revolver must have been pointed upwards at a slight angle. The setting of the weapon to aim at the brain of a man putting his head down on the pillow must have been a piece of very nice adjustment indeed.

"Did he always get into bed in such a way that the first thing he touched with the pillow was his head?"

"I — I've never seen him get into bed."

"If he'd sat on the pillow and then slid down under the sheet, he'd have been shot sideways through the buttocks."

"Yes, I suppose so. Of course, Jack How would have seen him get into bed, because they used to sleep on the veranda. But when I came here they'd moved into their rooms because the veranda roof leaks." He coloured under Spearpoint's doubting glance. "Of course, it hasn't rained in my time, but that's what Jack How told me."

"Any idea whose revolver this is?"

"It could be How's. He had a gun. He shot a pigeon with it, about three weeks ago. He was a cruel brute."

A car slithered into the compound. Spearpoint waved Anderton off the veranda; and while he was explaining the situation to Dr. Fell, Sub-Inspector Capel came charging up on his motor-bike, slung about with fingerprint apparatus and cameras. Leaving the two experts to their gruesome work, Spearpoint turned back to Anderton.

"Had your breakfast? I suppose not."

"I — I don't think I could eat. I told the cookboy he could go straight home after calling on you."

"You'll be all right when you get away from here. Some strong coffee would do you good. I want a chat with you, so you'd better come and have a bite at my place."

"I — I think I ought to go — somewhere else."

The young man turned away and was suddenly sick.

Spearpoint drove to his bungalow in silence, trying to sum up the jittery youth at his side. He knew Anderton as a newcomer to Malua, a quiet, respectable clerk, medium height, medium build, medium colouring — the sort of man who comes without exciting remark and is forgotten as soon as he goes. Age, about twenty-five. Unmarried, so far as was known.

Mrs. Spearpoint's coffee restored him

enough to make him venture on paw-paw and lemon, and egg on toast. The Inspector's breakfast was more substantial, as befitted a man with a teasing day's work ahead.

"Now tell me all you can think of that may have a bearing on this business."

"I don't know that I can tell you much. I wasn't there last night. But you know, don't you, that those two haven't spoken to each other for months? I didn't realise, until I came here, that two men could hate each other so much — share the same house and sit at the same table together three times a day, and never say a word."

"I know they came to blows three months ago. D'you mean to tell me they haven't spoken since?"

"That fight was before my time. In all the while I've been here, they only spoke to each other twice. All they normally did was to address obscene insults to each other through me. It was very — embarrassing."

"Did they threaten each other, or was

it just the sort of insult soldiers fling at each other?"

"It was usually just bawdy insults, under cover of talking to me. But once when I was there they almost started another fight. It was about a month ago, when I'd been working a bit late. When I came into the mess room they were shouting at each other across the table."

"What about?"

Anderton hesitated. "Well — I couldn't be sure; but I had the impression they were rowing over a girl."

"Who?"

"I wasn't sure. But Jack How was saying as I came up the steps, 'You keep your filthy hands off my girl!' And Boreman was sneering and roaring, 'Who says she's your something girl? If she was your something girl, I wouldn't use her for something practice!' Then they saw me, and dried up. But after the meal, Boreman got up and said grace in his usual style, 'If that's my something dinner, I've had it!' and went to walk out. He had to pass behind How, whose

16

chair was sticking out a bit, and he put his hands on How's shoulder and pushed him forward, and when he had passed, How turned quickly and stuck his foot out and hooked it round Boreman's ankle and tugged so that Boreman staggered; and Boreman got his balance and turned and clouted How on the side of the head. How was pinned against the table in his chair and couldn't dodge, but the blow sort of shifted him sideways — it was a real vicious swipe — and as he slid over he grabbed a knife. And the next minute he was on his feet, with the knife in his hand and his cheek beginning to bruise and a sort of grim smile on his face. And Boreman stood there with his fists clenched, snarling. I can't remember exactly what they said, but I know that How threatened, 'If you touch me again, I'll stick this in your fat belly!' and Boreman roared, 'You try! I'll twist your flaming neck!' "

"What happened then?"

"I thought How really was going to stab him. I made to get between them, but Boreman waved me away and went out. How put the knife down. He was shaking with rage."

"D'you think there was more to this feud than the fact that they'd been baching alone together for so long that they'd got on each other's nerves?"

"I'm pretty sure there must have been. When I came to the bach and found they weren't playing speaks, it seemed so silly that I tried to get them to act sensibly, but they wouldn't see reason. When I put it to How that if he couldn't get on with Boreman he'd be more comfortable at the hotel, he said he wasn't going to let that so-and-so drive him out; and when I tried to put it to Boreman, who was a rude hog of a man, he told me to mind my own something business, and when I pointed out that it was my business because it was misery sharing a home with two fellows who wouldn't speak to each other, he growled that if I didn't like living in the something bach I'd better go and live at the something hotel."

"Why didn't you?"

"I thought of it, but frankly, I couldn't afford it. I'm not on the same wicket as they were. It would cost at least a quid a week extra at the hotel, without counting taxis. You know, it's a mile from the store."

"But you slept at the hotel last night. Why?"

"I only went there for the night. How was having a party, and I thought they'd be pretty rowdy, and keep on to all hours, and I shouldn't get any sleep. Besides, the Fijians who've been unloading our timber ship were having a singsong, and drumming only a quarter of a mile away. So when How started up the gramophone, I made up my mind to go and get a good night's sleep at the hotel."

"Can you tell me who How's visitors were?"

Anderton mentioned five names, adding the obvious safeguard, "I don't know if anyone turned up after I left."

"You weren't invited?"

"I don't drink, you see. How did say

I could come in if I liked, but I've seen too much of that in the past, sitting there, stone cold sober, and watching the others getting redder and redder in the face and telling dirtier and dirtier stories. No good to me, so I cleared out."

"Did you have a quiet night at the pub? Saturday's usually a bit noisy there."

"It was at first, but my room was at the back, and they soon quietened down. I slept like a top."

Spearpoint, whose official residence was three hundred yards from the hotel and whose sleep had been interrupted by raucous singing from that direction well after midnight, accepted Anderton's statement without comment, and asked, "You really have no idea who the girl was they nearly fought over?"

Anderton hesitated just long enough to convince Spearpoint that he was about to lie. "No idea, I'm sorry."

"You said How claimed she was his girl. Did you know he had a girl?"

"He had a dozen!" Anderton's scorn

was obviously inspired by envy.

"But no particular one you know of?"

"No." Pressed for a list of the dozen, Anderton became evasive. He suggested some names, but he wouldn't like to swear in Court that any of these girls were the willing victims of his lust which How had proclaimed them to be. How often walked out in the evening with his rug over his arm and a girl's name on his lips, but he may have been only boasting.

"You haven't mentioned Barbara Villiers," Spearpoint objected. "I've seen her with him many a time."

Anderton flushed. Miss Villiers was the typist at Richmond, Lennox & Co.'s store, and therefore his companion during office hours. She was a tall, black-haired, blue-eyed quadroon in the early bloom of that voluptuous beauty which the mating of European and Melanesian stock so often produces. At forty, she would be enormous; but at nineteen, she was every man's desire. So far as Spearpoint knew (and it was his business to know everything discreditable about everyone on the Coast) she was virtuous.

Anderton's tone made it evident that he resented Jack How's familiarity with the girl. "Of course, they knew each other — working in the same firm. She's polite to everyone. She couldn't refuse to walk along the road with him if they happened to be going the same way, but he wasn't anything special to her."

Spearpoint thought: Evidently he was, and Anderton knows it. Aloud he asked, "Did he ever suggest he was?"

"He made salacious remarks about her, of course; but he exercised his filthy tongue about every girl in Malua."

Spearpoint decided to leave Anderton for the present under the illusion that his denial was accepted.

"Any idea where Boreman was last night?"

This put the clerk at his ease again. He answered with all the malice of the undaring envious. "I suppose he went to visit that woman he calls his rough island tabby. I don't know her name, or

22

where she lives."

"I think I know who you mean. Is there anything else you think you ought to tell me?"

"I don't think there is. Of course, I could tell you of a number of incidents — things they said about each other, and so on, but it wouldn't amount to more than that they hated each other like poison." He paused, and then went on with a rush. "Do you know what it looks like to me? I think they'd decided to murder each other. So How fixed up that booby trap to shoot Boreman as he put his head on the pillow; and Boreman, before he went to bed, sneaked into How's room and put the rug over his face until he stopped breathing. And then he got into his own bed — and Jack How shot him after he'd murdered Jack."

"So you think that's what happened, eh?"

"I can't see what else can have happened. After all, if someone wanted to murder them both, he'd either shoot them both, or smother them both, wouldn't he?

Besides, I can't think of anyone who'd want to murder them both. Boreman's the only chap in Malua who had it in for How."

"But not vice versa?"

"How certainly hated him as much as anyone."

"Was How the sort of man to fix up booby-traps?"

"He was rather. He was a motor mechanic. He used to mess about with old cameras and clockwork and things."

"I suppose you'll continue at the hotel for a time?"

Anderton shivered. "I wouldn't fancy going back to the bach — not yet, anyway."

"Did you have any plans for the week-end? Where can I find you if I want to ask you anything more?"

Anderton blushed, and then decided to confess like a man. "Actually, I was thinking of doing some painting this week-end — water-colour, you know. I thought of having a shot at those islands in the bay. I could do them from the hotel, if that's what you want."

"That'll be fine. I'll let you know as soon as I've searched the bach and you can get in to collect your stuff."

The young man seemed unduly perturbed at that; but Spearpoint judged him to be the sort of person who looks alarmed at any unexpected turn of events. Such a chap might look as dismayed at being prevented from fetching clean trousers from his room as a more stolid man would look on being caught pulling a knife out of a corpse.

2

Small Boy's Story

MR. TILSON, the manager of Richmond, Lennox & Co., was thoroughly impressed by the sense of his own importance that he took everything that happened on the West Coast of Viti Levu, and much that happened in the world Away, as directed personally at himself. Should a planter die or a mill mechanic's wife have a baby, or should the price of sugar or copra rise or fall in world markets, Mr. Tilson regarded the event as designed solely for the increase or decrease of his turnover.

Richmond, Lennox & Co., long established in Malua as timber merchants, had built up in recent years a respectable automobile supplies and repair business; so the manager was perhaps justified, on this sweltering Sunday morning, in the vindictiveness of his feelings against the criminal or criminals who had suddenly deprived him of the services of his timber-yard foreman and his motor mechanic. Spearpoint had to spend several minutes tactfully coaxing and flattering the unfortunate man before he could persuade him to concentrate on the needs of the police.

"I want to know anything you saw or heard last night which may help me to reconstruct events in the bach; and anything you can tell me about the men which may have a bearing on the affair."

Spearpoint did not expect Mr. Tilson would have much direct evidence to offer. R. L. & Co.'s compound was on rising ground on the west side of Malua Hill, so that the manager's house gave a wide view of the sea across the roof of the garage and timber shed; and the bungalows for the married men were also fairly well situated for breeze and aspect. But the bach was over the crest and shut

27

in by a thicket of wild lemon trees — a deliberate piece of town planning which suited everyone. Mr. Tilson was no fool, and he appreciated that if he wanted to keep a capable staff he would be wise to be blind to their leisure activities. He could sometimes hear, but never see from his house what went on at the bach; and a shady lane on the far boundary of the compound gave convenient and unobserved access for the bachelors and their visitors.

Mr. Tilson, fast asleep by eleven, knew nothing of last night's party beyond the fact that there had been some music from the direction of the bach.

His spouse had a great deal more to say. She confirmed, with understandable bitterness, that her lord and master had been snoring soon after eleven, but other noises had kept her awake until after one. The party had not disturbed her much; but about midnight a group of men, giggling drunk, had come through the compound and past the store on to the coast road. The natives in their temporary encampment on the shore had been banging their drums and singing long after that.

"There ought to be a law to stop them drumming on those *lalis* within earshot of a European house!"

"Did you hear a shot from the bach, Mrs. Tilson?"

"Yes, I did, but it was a long while after the party broke up — more than an hour, I should think. The *kaivitis* were still at their bawling, though."

Urged to try to remember more exactly what time she heard the shot, she presently suggested, "Ask the *kaivitis* what time they were singing *Isa Lei*. It was round about then. It was before they got on to *Abide With Me.*"

On the characters and backgrounds of the two men, Mr. Tilson could add little to what Spearpoint already knew.

Jack How came from Melbourne; he had been in the Islands, mainly Fiji and Samoa, for some five years, and with R. L. & Co. about eighteen months. His only known relative was a widowed mother who was, according to his story, both wealthy and obstinate; he gave out that he could not marry during her lifetime because she threatened that if he did, she would leave all her money to charity. Earlier in the year he had received a cable to say that his mother was dangerously ill, and had been granted a month's leave to bid her farewell. He had returned rather glum, saying the old lady had made a seemingly impossible recovery.

"You know, Inspector, as well as I do, that he didn't avoid female company when he was out of his mother's sight. Maybe he thought there was safety in numbers."

"You wouldn't say he had any special preference?"

"Since you ask me point-blank, I've suspected for a long time that there was something between him and Barbara Villiers. But would he have married the girl? Some men prefer a touch of the tar-brush. I wouldn't know. But, candidly, I'd be sorry to think Barbara wasn't a good girl. But who can guess what a girl will get up to? Of course, that cross-eyed little Carwell bitch is gone on him; he nosed around her till Barbara came."

Louise Carwell, the cashier at the store, was not cross-eyed, but she gave the impression of being so. She did not give the impression of being a bitch, though the way she looked at Jack How implied that she wanted to be.

Mr. Tilson could think of no reason why anyone should have murdered Jack How. Most people liked him. Boreman was the only person he'd rowed with, and Boreman rowed with everyone.

Joe Boreman, the doyen of the stall, with six years' service, was a valuable man because he could handle native labour. He swore at the *kaivitis* in Australian and jollied them along in their own language, and they laughed at him and obeyed him. He would be a flaming hard man to replace. He had come to Malua from Samoa, where he had left a part-native wife; no one knew if he contributed to her support. He had certainly found a series of substitutes in Fiji.

Most of the surviving inhabitants of the compound were standing in uneasy groups in the open space behind the manager's bungalow. As soon as the Inspector appeared they crowded round him, eager for assurances that this double murder on their doorstep was not the beginning of a crime wave that would engulf them all. Their anxiety was natural, for their veranda bungalows, if not fully open to the world, were easily entered.

Spearpoint told them bluntly that he did not yet know the sequence of events at the bach the previous night; but that his first impression was that the crimes had been planned and carried out by a European or part-European with reasons for killing either one or perhaps both of the victims; and that he had no reason to think that the rest of the compound had anything to fear. He did not believe there was a madman or a thief in the community who would presently strike again. However, he would keep a police guard on the bach and the compound until the matter had been cleared up. This was not entirely reassuring, but it was the best he could do; and they dispersed to their Sunday morning chores with expressions of gratitude or scepticism according to their natures.

The only man present who had attended How's party was Charlie Lyttleton, the building foreman, a precise little man with a frown. He owned to a headache, but Spearpoint suspected his ailment to be wife-displeasure.

"Of course I remember everything that happened last night, Inspector — perfectly. It was not a bender. Just a few friends having a yarn over a bottle of beer — a couple of bottles each, actually. Nothing vulgar. A feast of reason and a flow of soul. Naturally, we played records and sang a few songs. What's a party without the conviviality of joyous voices raised in harmony? As Shakespeare said, 'Dost thou think, because thou art virtuous, that there shall be no more cakes and ale?'"

Spearpoint took him by the arm and led him away so that he would stop trying to justify himself to his wife. "Look, I want to consult you about something in How's room. It's all right. The bodies have been removed."

In the heat of the morning, with minahs chattering in the eaves and doves cooing overhead, the deserted bach looked cool and therefore inviting. Inside, the only obvious sign of the tragedy which had happened there so recently was the reconnaissance party of ants, trailed across beds and floor, no doubt puzzled at the sudden disappearance of their prey.

In answer to questions, Lyttleton said that Boreman was not at the bach during the evening. Anderton remained in his room until he came to How's doorway about 8.30, knapsack in hand, and said he was going to the hotel for a night's sleep. He was not told they were breaking up at midnight. Two of the guests were mill mechanics who had to be on duty at six, one was a Catholic who never missed early morning Mass, and Lyttleton himself had promised his wife he would be home by eleven. The fifth guest was Harry Bennet, R. L. & Co.'s 'outside man', who passed out stone cold long before twelve. The other four carried him by arms and legs through the compound and dumped him on the front veranda of the store to cool off in the sea breeze.

"Was there anything unusual or strained in How's manner? Anything to make you think, looking back, that he was in any sort of apprehension or danger?"

"Not a thing, Inspector. Jack was his usual cheery self. Not a benighted care in the world."

"Any mention of his feud with Boreman?"

"Don't think so. Anyway, that didn't worry him — or Boreman either. They enjoyed it. The only beggar who was worried about it was young Anderton.

It was getting him down, all right, all right. And I don't wonder."

"Can you suggest anyone who had a grudge against How — a murderous grudge, I mean?"

"Absolutely no one, Inspector. Jack How was everyone's first choice for a drinking party or a day's fishing or what-have-you. But, of course, he did have what I may discreetly call 'other interests'. Not that I know any details. But, if it had been only poor Jack How who'd been murdered, and not Joe Boreman as well, I'd say *shareshay lar fum*. If you ask me who'd want to kill Jack How, Inspector, I'd say: some jealous female. You know what ladies are like when they get an idea into their heads. Hell hath no fury like a woman scorned, eh?"

"I wouldn't know. But I take your point. What about Boreman? Who'd want to murder him?"

"Rather ask: who wouldn't? There's such a thing as *day mortyouiss*, isn't there, Inspector? But even the icy fingers of death can't draw a veil over the fact that Joe Boreman had a shocking temper, and didn't care a sausage who he offended. But — " Lyttleton paused, looked away, shifted his feet, and then cleared his throat, and began, "Of course, there is one thing — " And stopped.

"Go on."

"Well, I suppose I must tell you this, Inspector. If I don't, you'll hear it from someone else, and then blame me for holding something back. But I wouldn't build too much on it if I were you. The fact is, poor old Harry Bennet was a bit — indiscreet last night."

"In what way?"

"Maybe you don't know that Mr. Tilson gave him the boot yesterday? He's been asking for it for a long time, of course, but it was Boreman who put his pot on — caught him bending over the count of the timber coming off the timber ship. Harry was tallying on the wharf but for two hours on Friday afternoon he was sleeping off his lunch in one of the holds, relying on the *kaiviti* boss boy to do the count. When Boreman got wind of this, he told Mr. Tilson he wouldn't work with that drunken so-and-so another day: either Bennet went out on his neck, or Boreman threw the job in. Didn't leave Mr. Tilson much option. There's poor old Harry's missus expecting number six any day, and what's his chance of getting another job? He's too well known. It's not that he drinks all that much. He can't hold it, that's his trouble. Mind you, there's nothing in this, Inspector. When he's sober, old Harry wouldn't squash a mosquito; and he was dead out when we left him last night. Even if he'd come to, he couldn't have held the gun steady."

Spearpoint cut through this apologia to ask bluntly, "Did he mention Boreman during the evening?"

"I'll say he did! That's the point. Everything was okey-doke until — about 10.30 or so. Then the beer got to working inside old Harry, and he treated us to a recital of his woes and wrongs. It was a bit off at a party, when everyone ought to be merry and bright, but we were all ready to weep sympathetic tears for him by that time; but we couldn't cheer him up. Never seen a man cry like he did. We just let him lie on the bed and sob himself out. Then he got up suddenly and grabbed a bottle, and staggered on to the veranda before we could stop him, shouting that he was going to bash that bastard Boreman. We yanked him back, but he wouldn't calm down until we'd taken him along to Boreman's room and shown him Boreman wasn't there. After that, he had another drink and then went dead out. Slid off his chair and thumped hard on the floor; and when we picked him up he was snoring. When we packed up an hour later, we couldn't wake him; that's why we left him on the porch to catch any breeze that was going."

"Why didn't anyone take him home?"

"You know he lives a ruddy mile away; the other chaps had to go in the opposite direction, and I couldn't carry him on my pat, even if I'd felt inclined. I was inclined more to bed than anything else just then; besides that, there was the ball and chain expecting me an hour before. But you needn't think that when old Harry came to, he toddled up to the bach and shot Boreman. He'd have been sober by then, and treading delicately all the way home in case he cracked a cockroach."

As they strolled back to Lyttleton's bungalow, Spearpoint asked if there had been any mention or sign of How's revolver during the evening.

Lyttleton replied that there had been no mention or sign of the revolver, but that everyone in the firm knew that How possessed it.

"Did you hear the shot?"

"Didn't hear a thing. I slept the sleep of the just."

His spouse had come on to the veranda in time to overhear this last (injudicious) remark, and corrected him bitterly, "Too drunk to hear anything, you mean."

Spearpoint diplomatically repeated his question to her. She asked angrily how anyone could have heard anything above the drum-banging and chanting of the natives on the beach. All she had heard from the bach was a lot of drunken bawling.

Ten-year-old Miss Lyttleton said she had heard a bang — a long time after her daddy had come home and her mummy had stopped talking to him. She had thought the bang a part of the Fijians' *meke,* a special effect on the *lalis* accompanying their national song, *Isa Lei.*

"Did you hear anyone moving about in the compound at the time?"

"No, Mr. Spearpoint. All I heard was the *kaivitis* on the beach."

As Spearpoint turned away, Lyttleton called him back.

"There's something I've just remembered, Inspector. It may be of some use to you. There was a woman asking for Boreman at the bach last night."

"Who was she?"

"You'll have to ask Jack How that. — Oh! silly of me! But he was the only one who saw her. It was — about ten o'clock, maybe. She called from the foot of the steps, 'Is Mr. Boreman there?' Jack went out to her. I wasn't listening to what he said. He was only out for a minute or two; when he came back he was grinning to himself, but all he said was, 'Old Boreman's rough island tabby had better watch out.' So it couldn't have been her."

Ernie Laws, the coachbody builder, was occupying Sunday morning in proper civilised style: cleaning his car. The exercise was not appearing to give him pleasure; but he explained that he had been awake all night with toothache. Mrs. Laws added the interesting fact that her husband's tooth-ache had kept her awake too.

They had both heard the shot, but they had thought it had come from the direction of the beach. The natives were singing *Isa Lei,* and Ernie had remarked that one drummer had been shot, and he wished they'd shoot all the rest and pack up their hullaballoo.

But after that the natives sang *God Be With You Till We Meet Again,* and *Abide With Me.* They had not noticed the time.

Ernie added that there had been a light in How's room for some time after the guests had left; he had thought nothing of that. Long after the shot, after the natives had packed up, Ernie had switched on the back veranda light, and had seen a man among the trees near the bach; he had thought nothing of that either. It was not uncommon for men to stroll through the compound at all hours of the night. Thinking it over in the light of the knowledge that two men had been murdered about that time, Laws decided that the figure had been more furtive, more disposed to keep under cover, than an honest man would have been. But he admitted that that had not been his impression at the time.

The Laws' bungalow was the nearest to the bach. In front of it, nearer the store, lived Bill Maitland, the chief clerk.

He greeted Spearpoint with, *"Siandra, turanga levu!* Here's the man who drove the bull through China without breaking a ruddy cup! Welcome to Bondi Beach! Mrs. M's been boiling the coffee for you for the last half-hour."

"I don't mind if I do."

Deck chairs on the shady veranda and hot sweat-inducing coffee gave the background to this interview, but it was dominated by the attempts of William Maitland Junior, an imaginative fourteen, to 'chime in'.

"What I want to know particularly was whether you heard or saw anything unusual last night."

"I did!"

"Keep quiet, William!" pleaded his mother.

"Whether you heard the revolver shot."

"I didn't hear the shot, but — "

"Keep quiet, William!"

" — but I did hear a bloodcurdling scream!"

"Oh, do be quiet, William. The trouble with this boy, Mr. Spearpoint, he's got

44

too much imagination, and he reads those horrible books."

"There was a yell, mummy; and they're not horrible."

"Let your father speak first."

Maitland put down his cup and said he had certainly heard a sound that might have been the shot. "And I can give you the good oil what time it was. About ten minutes later, I got up and poured myself a glass of cold water from the ice-chest. (Wonderful stuff; you ought to try it some time, Spearo.) The *kaivitis* were singing *Abide With Me,* and I was feeling ruddy glad I didn't have to. I happened to give a cork eye at the clock, and it was nineteen minutes past one. So you can bet the shot was about ten past — take or give a few minutes either way."

"Did you happen to notice if there was a light in the bach?"

"Can't see the bach from this place. Ernie Laws' joint's in the way."

"Can you remember what the natives were singing at the time of the shot?"

"Search me!" He searched his memory, but in vain. "They sang a hell of a lot of carols and hymns; and *Isa Lei*, of course. I think that was before *Abide With Me*."

"Did you hear anything, Mrs. Maitland?"

"I did! I heard a scream!"

"Be quiet when your mother's speaking."

"Well, I did hear a scream."

"If you don't pipe down," threatened his father, "we shall never hear you again."

Mrs. Maitland managed to get in that she had slept well and heard nothing.

Spearpoint turned to the boy.

"Tell me what you heard."

"I heard and saw everything. There was a man — "

"Don't take any notice of him, Mr. Spearpoint. He was dreaming in bed all night."

"I tell you I wasn't! I swear I saw a man walk past this house in the middle of the night."

"You mustn't swear, William."

"Father does."

46

His father promised him he could swear when he became a married man.

Spearpoint put in, "Let him tell his story."

"Something woke me up. I don't know what it was, honest. But I thought it was someone banging on the wall, outside. I got out of bed and looked out of the window, and there was this man going towards the bach. He was alongside Laws'. He wasn't walking straight. He was sort of staggering and stumbling. I saw him almost fall against a tree. He hadn't got a torch. I think he must have fallen against the house, and that was what woke me."

"How could you see all this?" his father asked. "It was as black as tar."

"I did so! I could see his white shirt and pants. And the light went on in Laws' back porch, and the man fell over a root, and went down, as if the light going on had shot him."

"Did you recognise him?" Spearpoint asked.

"No, I didn't. He fell over."

"Was he a European?"

"I thought he was; he was dressed like one."

"A big man?"

"Not very. About medium."

"This was long after the shot, wasn't it?"

"I didn't hear the shot," the boy admitted to his infinite regret — but to his credit, too.

"Were the Fijians still singing?"

"No, they weren't. Everything was quiet as quiet. All I could hear was the electricity engine."

"So you don't know what time this was?"

"No," with a reproachful glance at his father. "I haven't got a watch — yet." Then he brightened. "I got back into bed, and then I heard a terrible scream from the bach!"

"Really, William, you must learn not to make up these stories."

"But, mummy, there was a scream. It was a long bloodcurdling yell. I wonder it didn't wake up everyone."

48

"It didn't wake anyone up. You imagined it."

"Well, perhaps it wasn't such a scream as that," the boy conceded. "But it was a sort of — yelp; and it came from the bach. I'm telling you the truth, Mr. Spearpoint."

3

Dead Men's Stories

THE Indian cookboy at the bach was a dapper man with moustache too big for his face and a bald head. He was an excellent cook and he prided himself on wearing European clothes and on talking correct English.

"Good morning, Inspector. Yes; I have been employed on culinary duties in these bachelor quarters for almost five years."

"What were the relations between Mr. Boreman and Mr. How?"

"Extremely disputatious, Inspector."

"Did you ever see them quarrel?"

"Frequently, Inspector." Encouraged, the cook described the early morning fight over How's crooning, which he had seen partially through a crack in the wall between How's room and the kitchen. He

50

was unaware of Boreman's act of reprisal, but what he did describe with every air of truth was the argument over the girl which Anderton had interrupted.

"I was in the kitchen, preparing the evening repast. Their voices penetrated to the kitchen. The door was ajar and there was no avoiding over-hearing. They were both extremely angry. I inferred that Mr. Boreman had caressed a lady in the office in a manner which Mr. How considered unseemly and over-familiar." (Spearpoint, knowing Boreman, assumed that he had pinched the girl.) "It appeared that Mr. — How claimed some proprietorial rights in this female. Mr. Boreman maintained that he was not to be deterred from caressing the female when he wished to do so, whatever threats Mr. How might utter. He denied that the female could be considered to be Mr. How's property. He suggested that she was the property of 'the Boy Friend'."

"'The Boy Friend'? Oh Mr. Anderton?"

"Yes, Inspector; that is the sobriquet they employ when referring to Mr.

Anderton."

"Does he know that?"

"He is aware of it; and he is displeased; but he does not protest."

"Was he on friendly terms with either of them?"

"Certainly not, Inspector. Often he would not arrive for a meal until they had departed."

"Did he hear this quarrel?"

"The latter part of it."

"Do you know the girl they were quarrelling about?"

"It was the *Memsahib* Villiers, the stenographer at the store."

"Did Mr. Anderton know they were quarrelling about her?"

"Definitely, Inspector."

Spearpoint paused, and the Indian waited, deferential but fully relaxed.

"Did you know that Mr. How had a revolver?"

"Certainly, Inspector. The Sunday before last, he discharged it at a pigeon in that tree. Mr. Anderton was extremely distressed."

"Why?"

"The pigeon was not slain by the bullet. It fluttered to the ground, uttering dismal cries. Mr. How wrung its neck, and handed it to me for inclusion in a pie. But Mr. Anderton refused to partake of the pie."

"Did the sight of the blood make him faint?"

"He did not swoon, Inspector. He became pale and he retreated to his room. Mr. Boreman jeered at him."

The cook said he did not know where Mr. How had kept his revolver; it was no part of his job to look into the cupboards and chest-of-drawers in the rooms.

Dr. Fell drove bumpily into the compound. Spearpoint dismissed the cook and hurried over to the doctor.

The sun was now high. There was not a tremor of wind. The tall palms hung limp. Only mosquitoes and hornets had energy. From the Mission church by the wharf, the single bell was summoning worshippers to service. A peaceful Sunday morning — but not for Inspector Spearpoint.

"Been chasing you all over town, Spearo. Sooner those cadavers are under ground, the better. I can't tell you anything you don't know already. They were both pretty healthy specimens. Boreman's liver would have played up if he'd lived for another ten years' steady drinking. Nothing the matter with How, except lack of breath at the end."

The doctor then entered into technicalities which boiled down to the facts that How had been suffocated and that Boreman had been shot through the brain; both had died about one a.m. It was impossible to say who had died first.

"There's one thing I ought to point out to you, Spearo, though you've probably noticed it yourself. It's your field rather than mine. All How was wearing was canvas shoes and pyjama trousers. Incidentally, he'd bitten at that rug; that did the job all right. Boreman was wearing pyjama trousers and the dirty shirt he'd been wearing all day."

"I did notice that, Fell. The pyjama

jacket was hanging on the door. Maybe he was too drunk or too lazy to change the shirt. Anything in the pockets?"

"Not a thing. The left one was unbuttoned."

Dr. Fell went off to play a round of golf before lunch, and Spearpoint began a systematic search of the bach while waiting for Sub-Inspector Capel to arrive with the results of his finger-printing and photography.

With the aid of the keys in the dead men's pockets, Spearpoint studied what he could of their private lives. But he found hints rather than facts. Neither man was given to hoarding papers.

In the wallet locked in his trunk, How had a passport, a licence for his revolver (bearing the number of the weapon in Boreman's room), a savings bank book with a moderate balance, and some Tasmanian sweepstake tickets. There were a few references and papers relating to his employment with R. L. & Co. What was more interesting was a bundle of postcard photographs and snapshots. Nearly all were either 'Jack How' or 'Jack How with Girl'. Six of these relics of past sunshine seemed to Spearpoint to be particularly important. A snapshot of How with an elderly lady who was presumably his mother; a postcard photograph of the same lady, signed 'Your loving mother'; a snap of How in a suburban garden with his arm round a fluffy-haired young lady; a snap of the same lady, with a baby in her arms and a girl toddler at her side, endorsed, 'Love from Nelly and Little Nell. Is he like his father?'; a Sydney studio portrait of Barbara Villiers, inscribed, 'Ever yours, Barbara'; and, finally, a street photographer's postcard of Barbara and How, arm-in-arm and smiling, with Sydney Harbour Bridge in the out-of-focus background.

The only letters How had kept were two recent ones from 'Mother' and 'Nelly', both writing from Melbourne. Spearpoint thought it likely that How had intended to destroy them when he had answered them, since there was no obvious reason why they should have been preserved. Mother's was a little pathetic, expressing anxiety at not hearing from her son for more than two months, and hope that he had not been ill. It did not read at all like the letter of a wealthy and dominating woman. The only reference to money was:

"The rents were rather slow in coming in this quarter, and I couldn't send Nelly anything until last week. She was glad to have it, because Jacky has been a bit crook, but he's all right now, and she has a better job, so you need not worry about her."

There was no evidence that Jack How had been worrying about Nelly or about anyone else. Nelly herself had written five pages of gossip about the children's health, the weather, her job in a department store, and the doings of various friends. She, too, referred to the rents:

"My money was late this quarter, I didn't get it until the 20th, but Mum said the rents were late, and so long as I get it in the end, I can manage O.K."

The only personal note in this 'Dear Jack' — 'Love Nelly' letter was a plea to him to throw up his job and come back to Melbourne. "I'm sure you'd like to see the children, and little Nell is always talking about you and asking when you're coming home again."

It was, thought Spearpoint, a nice sisterly letter.

The search of How's room took some time, for he was a dressy man, and a man interested in his trade. But Spearpoint found nothing of interest hidden among the clothes, or under the piles of technical publications and the mechanical parts in the cupboard. The only item that seemed to have a bearing on the crimes was the half-empty box of revolver cartridges on the top shelf of the cupboard.

There was perhaps some significance in the fact that the liquor cabinet was unlocked and empty, with the key in the lock. On the West Coast, men guarded their whisky both from pilfering servants and from raiding cobbers; and the drinking man never drained the last drop on a Saturday night — especially on the Saturday before Bank Holiday.

Boreman's six year occupation of the room at the other end of the bach had left singularly little trace. But his hobbies were beer and women, which mark a man's body rather than his habitation. There were half-a-dozen of beer in his padlocked ice-chest, and an empty beer bottle near the door. Spearpoint thought it likely that Boreman had drained this before getting into bed; if so, he must have thrown the bottle-top into the compound: it was not lying about in the room.

Boreman's few papers included a passport, a savings bank book and some tickets in Tatts; but no gun licence. A notebook recorded transactions with a bookmaker in Brisbane, not unduly unprofitable. These records, together with a few personal papers and books of racing form, were jumbled in disorder in a locked suitcase which was the only piece of luggage in the room. Boreman evidently travelled, and lived, light. His few well-worn clothes were in the chest-of-drawers. There were no photographs, and, what was more strange, no money. Even in a land where everyone runs up monthly bills, men usually carry the price of an occasional drink or taxi. How had left about six pounds in cash.

Capel arrived with his photographs, which were merely excellent records, and his fingerprint report, which added to the policemen's knowledge.

With the involuntary and voluntary co-operation of the four normal users of the bach — Boreman, How, Anderton and the cook — Capel had obtained samples of their prints and matched them with impressions on articles in the building. On the tumblers and empty bottles in How's room were prints no doubt left by his five guests. These would have to be verified. Around the lock and lid of Boreman's suitcase were traces of a tenth person. The revolver and the surfaces ancillary to the booby-trap bore no marks at all. But on top of the neat pile of clean shirts in the open drawer was a rumpled blue silk handkerchief, smelling faintly of perfume, which might have been used to hold the revolver and wipe out marks elsewhere.

Spearpoint and Capel spent some time trying in vain to jam the revolver at a suitable angle in the open drawer, and considering how it had been fired. The cord, with one end tied to the trigger, went under the pillow and was tied to the bed-post at the far side, some twelve inches lower. The theory apparently was that the cord, stretched tight, raised the pillow slightly, so that when Boreman put his head down, the trigger was pulled.

"We'll have to give a bit of thought to this," Spearpoint remarked. "The only thing that seems clear at the moment is that the gink who rigged this up is either a ruddy fool, or he took us for ruddy fools."

"Probably both, sir."

"Of course, there may be more in this than appears on the surface; the joker's either very clever indeed, or too clever by half."

"There's a point that's occurred to me, sir: if this stretched cord is all my eye and the murderer really shot him in the usual way, wouldn't he have to be left-handed to get a shot in from between the chest-of-drawers and the bed?"

"Squeeze yourself in there and see if you can shoot with your right hand."

Capel tried. It was a tight fit, but Capel was tall and had to bend down to shoot upwards.

"Someone slender and short could fit in to fire right-handed, sir — just."

"Slender and short, eh? That reminds me, there's just time before lunch for you to buzz down to the hotel and bring Anderton up to collect whatever he needs for a day or two. Keep as close a watch as you can on what he takes without making it too obvious."

"Shall I try to find out if he's left-handed?"

"Look for it; but don't ask him."

The landlord of the *Don Bradman* hotel confirmed that Anderton had booked a bed a little after nine last night. "He reckoned there was a sing-song at the bach and a *meke* on the beach, and he wanted a quiet night."

"Did he get it?"

"My oath he did! Bill Crofts got a wire yesterday to say he'd won five hundred bits of bumpf in Tatts, and he had half the mill celebrating in the bar here till I threw 'em out at eleven; then they kept it up on the beach across the road until two."

"I heard 'em. They keep you awake?"

"I'll say! But what's the odds? They'd spent a few quid in the bar, and the beach here's the only place where they're not keeping the whole burg awake. There's only the Mission and the Civil Service within earshot, and who cares about them? I left the porch lights on, and they gathered round the old boat and didn't let up while the booze lasted."

"Did Anderton have a room on that side?"

"No fear! I gave him one on the backside. But he'd have heard 'em all right, all right!"

"Did he complain?"

"Nope; but he keeps his tongue padlocked, that lad."

"May I see the room, please?"

"Sure thing; he's there now. Came back about nine, saying the other two in the bach had been murdered last night, and could he have the room so that people wouldn't keep pestering him with questions about it. Your side-kick took him up to the bach to get some duds, and after lunch he went up to the room and stuck there." Anderton had given only the barest facts and refused to say more, pleading that it gave him the horrors to think of what he had seen. The news of the murders had been spread in the township by the Indian cook, who had not, however, seen the bodies.

The hotel was a two-storey wooden building, with business premises on the ground floor and domestic offices above. A balcony ran round three sides of the upper storey, with one staircase leading down inside the building to the dining-room, and another leading outside to the back of the hotel. The room Anderton occupied was close to the outside staircase.

Spearpoint glanced in, saw that Anderton was lying on the bed reading, apologised briefly for the intrusion, and withdrew. On the way down, the landlord's wife assured Spearpoint that the bed had been slept in.

Spearpoint's next calls took him to the two mill mechanics and the Catholic who had been at How's party; their stories differed in minor details from Lyttleton's, but corroborated it in all points the police were interested in. All agreed that the revolver had not been mentioned or displayed. Only one had clearly heard the voice of the woman who had called for Boreman, and he had thought she had sounded like a part-European.

Harry Bennet lived in the unfashionable suburb of Althorp, a mile or so on the road to Ba. His ramshackle bungalow really belonged to his wife, who had inherited it from her half-English father. The place swarmed with native and partly-native children. No one in Malua wondered why Harry could not keep off the drink.

Spearpoint found his first real check at Bennet's house. For Mrs. Bennet, forty-odd, and without a trace of the lissom grace which had captivated the young Harry, and now particularly ungainly as she bore the evidence of her submission to him, was a very worried woman. Her husband had not been home since he went off to Mr. How's party, and she had no idea where he was. She was absurdly anxious. To her, he was not a good-for-nothing drunk and waster who, now that he had lost his job, would be a burden rather than a support; he was her man; it was even possible that she still loved him; she was very afraid she might never see him alive again.

4

The Rough Island Tabby's Story

AT the Police Station, Spearpoint found an urgent message from Mr. Tilson:

'Come here at once. Important news for you.'

Spearpoint had no more taste than the next man for being ordered about, but this set him driving full tilt to R. L. & Co.'s compound.

Somewhat to his surprise, he found it thronged with Fijians — huge, chocolate-coloured men and women, with upstanding fuzzy hair. There seemed to be scores of them, but in fact there were about fifty, standing and sitting in front of the store, and all in their Sunday best: the men in silk shirts and clean white sulus, the women in shapeless long dresses in primary colours. A few had white limed hair, and the smell of their coconut oil hair-dressing was almost overpowering. Like most native gatherings, the crowd appeared good-humoured and patient; but there was an air of anxiety about their idleness, and Spearpoint was puzzled to observe that his arrival was greeted with relief.

Some of the women hailed him with *"Mbula!"*, in tones which made it sound more like 'Hurrah!' than 'Good day!', and giggled when he returned the salutation.

A very harassed-looking manager stood on the veranda, with two large natives squatting hopefully at his feet. He hurried down the steps to greet Spearpoint, a sure sign that he was thoroughly upset.

He was indeed so angry that though his mouth opened and shut, no words came.

"What's up?"

Mr. Tilson managed to stammer out that Boreman had drawn the cash on Saturday to pay this labour, and now it couldn't be found. "W-w-what's he d-d-done with it, eh?"

"I don't know — yet," Spearpoint retorted, stolidly.

"Then you'd b-b-better find out, hadn't you, d-d-damned quick? These boys w-w-want to g-g-get off home."

"I shall find out everything in due course, Mr. Tilson. But I shan't find anything out any quicker for your bawling at me. I have already come to the conclusion that Boreman's room was burgled last night. Who are these boys and how much do they want?"

Mr. Tilson calmed down sufficiently to explain that the assembled natives were the entire able-bodied male population of the village of Mataiveithangge, thirty miles away in the mountains of the interior (with many of their womenfolk and children in tow), who had contracted to unload the timber-ship *Frances Teresa* during the past week, and had now come for their pay: £147.10.0. Boreman had drawn it from the bank on Saturday morning, intending to pay it out at lunch-time, but the head man, the *turanga ni koro,* had asked him to hold it until Sunday, because they were having a sing-song on Saturday night and not departing for home until Sunday afternoon.

The Fijians crowded round. Those who understood English interpreted to the others, and from time to time a little chorus of assent or approbation arose. *Vinaka! Vinaka!* (Good! Good!) It was the truth the boss was telling the Inspector.

When Mr. Tilson had finished, the *turanga ni koro* broke in and explained everything again in Fijian; and more choruses of admiring approbation confirmed the story.

Then there was silence. Everyone looked at Spearpoint expectantly, as if they took it for granted that he would produce the money from inside his helmet.

But Spearpoint disappointed them. He thanked the *turanga ni koro* courteously in the native tongue, and then drew Mr. Tilson aside.

"I've searched Boreman's room, and there isn't a note or a coin there. It may be he had some secret hiding-place, but before I tear the whole building to pieces in search of it — are you sure he didn't put the money anywhere in the office?"

"He didn't come into the office."

"Could he have given it to someone else to put in the safe, or somewhere else in the office?"

"He could not! I gave him the cheque the last thing before I locked the safe; and by the time he came back from the bank, the store was locked."

"What about his desk in the timber-shed?"

"He hasn't got a desk — just a table."

"What do you suppose he did with the money?"

"How the hell should I know? I'm asking you."

"It's no use getting excited. The stuff's lost for the moment, but it must be somewhere."

"You'd better look smart and find it. These boys want to get off home."

"That's your responsibility, not mine.

The best thing you can do is to draw another lump from the bank and pay the football team off."

"How the hell can I draw money from the bank on a Sunday afternoon?"

"That's up to you, Mr. Tilson."

"It's up to you to find the damn money!"

"You're talking like a fool, Mr. Tilson, and that's not like you. You know damn well that the responsibility for paying these boys is yours. If you entrusted cash to a member of your staff and he's lost it, the loss is your firm's. I'll do what I can to recover the money but you can't expect me to produce it out of my hat."

"All right, all right, all right," grumbled the harassed timber merchant. "I thought you'd have known what happened to the money."

Spearpoint, who had no doubt that the bank manager would open up to oblige his Saturday night bridge partner, turned away, and beckoned to the *turanga ni koro.*

When and where, he asked in Fijian, was Mr. Boreman asked to keep the money until Sunday?

It was just after the office was locked up.

Did he say what he would do with the money?

He said he'd keep it in a safe place; he put it in the breast pocket of his shirt.

Where did this conversation take place?

On the veranda of the store.

Was any other European present?

Yes. Harry Bennet. The young turanga who locked the door of the store might have heard, too; he was waiting to get past the group at the top of the steps.

Mr. Tilson butted in with, "He means Anderton. He locked up as usual and brought me the key before that; I sent him back to fetch my jacket which I'd left on the bench here."

Spearpoint dismissed the Fijian, and remarked, "So Anderton and Bennet knew that Boreman had the money. And Bennet has disappeared."

"Disappeared?"

73

"He was at How's party last night, and drunk himself to sleep. They left him on the porch here, and he's not been seen since. By the way, you sacked him yesterday?"

"He's had it coming to him for a long time. I've warned him till I was sick of warning him. He was dead drunk in the hold of the *Frances Teresa* when he should have been tallying this timber."

"They say on the beach that it was a complaint from Boreman that finally put his pot on."

The great Mr. Tilson was not standing for that insinuation. "Nothing of the kind. Whoever told you that should mind his own damned business. Boreman reported that Bennet was not carrying out his duty, as was only right and proper. But I dismissed Bennet because I'd given him a final warning a fortnight before."

"Thanks. Glad to have the story straight." Spearpoint hoped he sounded as if he believed it. "Now, I'd better leave you with your problem and I'll get back to mine." Waving, and calling *"Sa mauthe"* (Farewell) and *"Vakamalua"* (Take it easy) to the *Kaivitis*, he got back into his car, and, to their evident disappointment, drove off along the coast.

"Did Mr. Boreman visit you on Saturday evening?"

"Mr. Boreman? Why should he visit me?"

"That's no business of mine, but — "

"No, it isn't, Mr. Spearpoint; so why ask?"

"I have to trace his movements on Saturday."

"It's no good asking me. I didn't even know him."

Spearpoint kept his temper but changed his tactics.

"That's a pity. I thought he was a friend of yours."

"Whoever told you that was no friend of mine."

"I'm sorry. You see, he appears to have been a rather lonely man. He didn't have a lot of friends. I thought he came here sometimes to spend an evening in congenial company."

"We don't have that sort of company here, Mr. Spearpoint. This is a respectable house, I'd have you know."

"That was what I thought. What I meant was: he came here to spend a quiet evening among friends."

"It was never a quiet evening when he came here. He put on the gramophone and sat listening to it all the damn evening. Sat with a silly grin on his face listening to the comics all the damn evening."

"That's all, eh?"

"What d'you mean: that's all? What else do you think he came for? I've got the best collection of comics in the Colony."

"So I've heard say. Well, it's a pity he didn't come here to listen to them last night, because when he got home from wherever he went, he was murdered; and if I could find out where he was and what time he left, and so work out what time he might have got back to the bach, I might be able to find out who murdered him."

"If that's all you want to know, Mr. Spearpoint, he left here just before midnight."

"You're sure it was just before midnight?" The walk to the bach would have taken him some twenty minutes.

The girl was insistent on the point. "Certain sure. And for why? My mother always made him go at twelve; she says she won't have the dregs of one day staying in the cup for the next."

"Thanks. One other thing: what was he wearing?"

"The clothes he always wears, of course. You know better than a girl like me what clothes a man wears."

"Was he wearing a white shirt with two breast pockets?"

"Never seen him in anything else."

"And can you remember whether he had anything in the pockets?"

"Do you think I pry into his pockets?"

"Now, look!" Spearpoint implored her, patiently. "Don't think I'm accusing you of anything, but I must get at the truth. I know that earlier in the day he had a large sum of money in his shirt pocket; and I want to know if he hid it somewhere in the bach, or whether he kept it in his pocket all the evening."

The girl was not such a fool as she pretended to be. She answered at once, with evident truth. "He had it in his pocket. He said he'd got to keep his eye on that shirt, because he had a lot of money in the pocket. And the pocket bulged a lot. He made a stupid joke about it. And he still had the money in his pocket when he went home. You won't find any money in this house."

"Did he take his shirt off during the evening?"

She stared at him in well-feigned surprise. "What the devil would he want to take his shirt off for, Mr. Spearpoint?"

"It was a hot evening."

"Yes, that's right. It was a hot evening. He took his shirt off and folded it carefully with the money pocket inside and put it under his trousers."

"You mean he sat on it?"

"Never you mind what I mean, Mr. Spearpoint. All I'm saying is, he brought the damn money here where he knew it'd be safe, and he took it away again."

Spearpoint got up. "That's fine. That's exactly what I wanted to know. I was pretty certain he had the money in his pocket when he got into bed at the bach, but I wanted to make sure he carried it about with him all the evening."

"He did so." The girl got up. "I'm sorry he's dead. Sensible, that's what he was. Why don't you come along one evening, eh? I've got the best lot of comics in the Colony; make you split your shirt laughing."

"I'm afraid that's not very much in my line."

"You never know what's in your line till you try, you know," she urged. "Every man likes a bit of good clean fun. Good clean fun, that's what you'd get here."

"Yes, that was what I understood."

A brief interview with the girl's mother

confirmed her story: Mr. Boreman always went ('like a damn lamb') just before the new day began.

"I expect Mr. Tilson has told you that the cash drawn by Boreman yesterday afternoon to pay the *Frances Teresa* labour is missing?"

The bank manager indicated that he had been dragged out of his Sunday afternoon nap to furnish a repeat.

"It was £147.10.0?"

"Exactly."

"How was it made up?"

"All in pound notes, bar one for ten bob."

"Can you give me any numbers to trace them by?"

"We don't note the numbers, of course; but I'd know four of 'em again. One has my own bundle total on it you know, what's left in a hundred after I've broken into it. It's 44. I gave him this forty-four, an unopened hundred and three throw-outs."

"Throw-outs?"

"Defaced notes I'd put aside. One with

'God send you back to me' scribbled on it in red ink — in vain, no doubt; one rather disloyal one with a moustache inked on the Sovereign's face; and a torn one stuck together with stamp paper."

"I thought you didn't pay out defaced notes?"

"There you're poking into one of the mysteries of banking, Spearo. If you find those notes, you'll be glad I paid 'em out, won't you?"

Capel, having persuaded the four available guests at How's party to provide fingerprints, had identified their tumblers; and assumed that the prints on another tumbler must be Harry Bennet's. The same prints were on a bottle which appeared to have been held by the neck 'as if to bash someone with', and on the empty bottle in Boreman's room.

But an unidentified print on Lyttleton's tumbler proved that some as yet unidentified person — and not the one who had been at Boreman's suitcase — had been in How's room and drunk from a used tumbler.

The village barber, trudging home from an Indian festivity, swore that he had passed Boreman going towards the bach at ten past twelve — nearly an hour before his death.

5

Barbara Villiers' Story

"HERE'S a quick one for you, Lyttleton. When you came away from How's, was there any liquor left?"

"We finished the beer. Jack insisted on that. 'Can't leave one bottle', was his clarion cry. There was about an inch of whisky left for Sunday. And he said he had a full flask of brandy in the cupboard."

"You know I've had a couple of Mohammedan constables on guard since 8.30. Does it surprise you to be told there's not a drop of liquor in the room now?"

"Jack might have finished the Scotch; there was only about an inch. But a flask of brandy!"

"The empty flask isn't there, either."

"We never saw it. Jack may have been kidding when he said he had a flask full in the cupboard."

"Can you give me another minute, Mr. Maitland?"

"I shall be delight-eded."

"Can you tell me why Harry Bennet was sacked?"

"You'd better ask the boss that, Inspector."

"I don't want Mr. Tilson's reasons. I want to know what the staff thought were his reasons. How far was it Boreman's doing?"

"About as far as from here to eternity, I should say. Look! It was about eleven yesterday morning. Boreman and Bennet staged a ceremonial procession through the store and the office into Mr. Tilson's room. Boreman was shouting in one of his ten-high rages. You know what he was like! The only difference between Boreman and a raging lion is that Boreman was clean-shaven. I told him to cut out the rough stuff in front of Barbary

Villiers — not that she hadn't heard all the words before often enough, but I like a bit of decency in the office when I'm in charge. Harry was trotting along behind with his tail between his legs and a gushing stream piling up behind his eyelids. The guts of Boreman's broadcast was that he'd had his bellyfull of old Harry, that Harry was going out on his sanguinary neck, and if his wife and kids starved they'd be sanguinary lucky to be rid of Harry.

"Someone shut the door of Mr. Tilson's room, but I guess you heard Boreman at the Police Station. It's not much more than half-a-mile away. In his delicate way, he was trying to insinuate that Bennet had been slightly un-sober when he should have been tallying timber; that Boreman would, on the whole, rather prefer, perhaps, not to work with him any more; and that if the manager was not willing to give some tentative consideration to the possibility of suggesting to Bennet that he might think of looking for alternative employment, Boreman might perhaps be inclined to think of making a move himself. We didn't hear what the others said; but after about five minutes Boreman came out and I told him off for using such language in the office. He just laughed and turned to Barbary. She was over at the filing cabinet, and he said, 'She likes it, don't you, lovey?' and gave her a pinch. She was asking for it, turning her back on him, I admit. But she swung round, furious, and shouted, 'No, I don't!' and gave him a terrific slap round the ear-hole. She's a hefty wench, as you know, and she's got great tennis-smash arms and hands on her, and it staggered him. For a moment I thought he was going to knock her down. So I moved over and told them to cut it out. He gave a grin and strolled out. His cheek was a ruddy sunset. She was upset, though — My God!"

"What's the matter?"

"I've just remembered. Perhaps I ought not to be telling you this. It might put ideas into your head. But someone else might tell you. You know she's a good kid."

"You'd better explain."

"She said, 'I'll murder that swine if he doesn't stop pinching me!' But it slipped my memory until now, because poor old Harry came out of Mr. Tilson's office then, and he was really weeping this time. He'd found his tongue, too; but I hadn't the heart to tell him off."

"Did he utter any threats against Boreman?"

"Not that I remember. He certainly put the blame on Boreman. He seemed chiefly concerned about his old woman. Is it number eight or number nine she's expecting?"

"Only the sixth; but, with nephews and nieces and whatnots, there are more than a dozen kids swarming round that home, and he's the sole support."

"Then he ought to take care of his job, oughtn't he? But I suppose that's what drives him to the booze."

"It would be. Was Anderton in the office when all this happened?"

"Too right. He kept mum, but I could see he'd have given quids to have had the guts to knock Boreman down. He's as potty over Barbary as Barbary was over Jack How."

"Was that really serious — on both sides?"

"It was on hers. I can give you the good oil on that. You'd only got to see the way she looked at him. When he came into the office, she'd sit up and follow him round with her eyes. You'd think he was a hero of the first water, second water, bath water, *and* waste-pipe. He jollied her along, but she was just one of seventeen to Jack How."

"Did she realise that?"

"I don't reckon she did. I warned her more than once. After all, she's a decent kid; someone ought to talk to her like a father sometimes. I said to her, 'Look here, Barbary, you don't want to get too serious with gay Jack How. He's not the marrying kind. If you're not careful, he'll let you down with a bump.' But she wouldn't take that from me or anyone else. She knew she wasn't the only orange in the basket, but he kidded her she was on top. She reckoned he'd promised to marry her when his mother pegged out. You've heard that yarn about the jealous ma with her hands folded over the money-bags? Believe it or not! I told Barbary she was a fool to rely on his puff-ball promises, but she reckoned she could take care of herself. That's how girls go wrong. When I said I hated to see a nice girl like her being led up the garden, she giggled and said it was a lovely garden. I told her she hadn't reached the end of it yet. Suppose he locked her in the tool-shed and married someone else. She said, 'He wouldn't do that. I've promised him that if he ever did that I'd cut his lying throat.' She didn't mean that, though, Spearo. She was laughing. She didn't mean it seriously."

"I know the way girls say things like that. One other thing: can you tell me anything about How shooting a pigeon in the compound some Sundays ago?"

"It was one Sunday afternoon, about three weeks back. The damned fool winged it with his revolver. It had perched on that tall tree over there, and it slipped down, fluttering and squawking. It tried to fly and couldn't, with a broken wing; and it screamed, rather horribly. It got caught in a branch, and then fell to the ground. How wrung its neck and gave it to the cook for a pie."

"You saw it fall?"

"I heard the shot and then I heard someone screaming. So I hurled myself on to the veranda to see what the hell was up. Young Anderton was bawling louder than the bird. How picked it up still struggling, and when the Boy Friend screamed at him, he swung it round as if he was going to hit him in the face with it. Some of the blood did spatter over him. Anderton turned to run away, and collided with Boreman, and they both jeered at him."

"Did the sight of the blood make him faint?"

"I'm not sure. He didn't faint. He

said next day that the thought of the tormented bird made him sick. He was hysterical. I reckon he was dead scared. It took him days to get over it."

Barbara Villiers was lovely to look at. There was no disputing that. The native quarter of her ancestry had given her a strong, splendid and well-proportioned body; the Irish three-quarters had given her shapely features, blue eyes and glossy hair. What was not so evident was the blend of ancestry in her character. Away from the Islands, certainly in the green island her father came from, few would have suspected, from either her appearance or her manner, that her blood was mixed. But when one of your grandmothers was a half-naked savage, and the man she bore your mother to was a roving trader; and when your father, too, was a rolling stone who had been miner, soldier, sailor, farmhand and a dozen other things — then the veneer of your New Zealand boarding school education must certainly conceal passions and impulses which threaten to destroy your attempts to be a civilised lady. However she dressed and carried herself, it must be expected that her native ancestors had bequeathed her something more than large hands and feet.

But, thought Spearpoint as he looked at her, it is a mistake to think of the Fijians as merely the most savage warriors of the Pacific; the Fijians were also an honest and honourable race, with a code of loyalty and kindliness.

He treated her with grave politeness, which was no doubt a welcome change from the patronising jollying along she had to endure from most European men.

"Thank you for coming here so promptly, Miss Villiers. Please sit down. Do you smoke?"

"No, Mr. Spearpoint. Thank you." Her expression as she sat down and pulled her skirt over her knees defied them to regard her as anything but a business visitor.

"I don't know if you can help us at all, Miss Villiers, but I've asked you along because I have to find out exactly what happened at the bach last night, and I'm trying to discover who might have been there after Mr. How's party broke up. So I'm asking everyone who knew Mr. How and Mr. Boreman at all well what they can tell me about their habits, friends, and enemies."

She listened frowning, looking down at the floor. Once she opened her mouth as if to interrupt, and then thought better of it. When he paused, she remained silent.

"If you would tell me anything you think might help, and I think it might be useful, Sub-Inspector Capel will write it down, and I'll get you to sign it."

She looked up then, candidly. "What do you want me to say, Mr. Spearpoint? Everybody knows I was friendly with Mr. How, and everybody knows I didn't like Mr. Boreman. But I don't know any more than anyone else who their friends or enemies were — except that I don't think Mr. How had any enemies. Of course, I'm very sorry indeed about Mr. How — " She broke off, her voice trembling; but pulled herself together. "I can't say I'm sorry about Mr. Boreman, because I don't suppose anyone can be sorry about him. But what else I can say, I don't know."

"I understand you had a set-to with Mr. Boreman in the office yesterday morning?"

"He pinched me; and I slapped his face," she conceded, simply. "I'm not sorry I did either, though he's dead now. He deserved it. I hit him as hard as I could, and I hope it hurt. Am I supposed to be sorry?"

"I don't see why you should be. How friendly were you with Mr. How?"

She hesitated, and then smiled at him frankly. "There was nothing — wrong, if that's what you mean. I went out with him in the evenings sometimes, but he wasn't the man to be satisfied with one girl." Her tone was enigmatic. Spearpoint could not tell whether she was malicious or indifferent.

"I'm sure he wasn't constant to you," he assured her, brutally. "But did you really care?"

Suddenly, her composure gave way. Her eyes filled with tears, and she looked down at the floor, biting her lips.

They waited while she took a handkerchief from her bag and wiped her eyes. Then she looked up, smiling crookedly.

"I'm sorry. You see, I really was fond of him."

"Of course." Having made his point, he spoke more gently. "When did you see him last?"

"Yesterday morning, when the store closed."

"You didn't see him later that day?"

She shook her head, still emotional. "I may as well admit it: we'd had some words. Saturday was the anniversary of the day we first went out together, and I said we must do something special, and he thought I meant — I mean, he pretended to misunderstand me; and in the end, he said that if I wanted

95

a Special Saturday Evening, I'd better stay at home; he would have a beer — up at the bach. So I played tennis in the afternoon, and after that I went home."

"You had a holiday in Australia this year?"

"Yes, I did," she conceded, looking down at her shoes.

"Mr. How was in Australia at the same time?"

"Yes, he was."

"Did you see anything of him there?"

He wondered if she would lie, but she looked up at him quite calmly and admitted, "Yes, we had a week together in Sydney. I was staying with a girl I'd been to school with in Auckland, and she married an Australian, and invited me to Sydney for a holiday. Jack — Mr. How — went to Melbourne because his mother was ill, but when she recovered he came to Sydney for a week. It was nice to be able to go about together without feeling that people were watching us all the time."

"Where did he stay?"

"At a hotel. I don't know the name. He used to call for me at my friend's and bring me back there." She gave her friend's address.

"Did you meet his mother?"

Barbara laughed. "Oh, no. She's one of these possessive mothers. He's — I mean, he was scared of her. She wouldn't let him marry. She'd have cut him out of her will. Besides, she lives in Melbourne."

"Was there any suggestion that he would have married you but for his mother?"

She did not answer for a moment. Then she confessed, simply, "Yes, I'm sure he would. I would have married him. I didn't care about the money."

"I suppose now he's dead, all the money will go to his sister?"

She looked doubtful. "I didn't know he had a sister."

"Apparently she's married and lives in Melbourne, too." She made no comment on that, and Spearpoint wondered what else to ask. She had spoken with frankness

97

and every air of truth, and yet he was not quite satisfied. He felt there was something behind her words that he must get at.

"Are you at all friendly with Mr. Anderton?"

"Not outside the office. He's all right there."

"Is there anything else you think I ought to know that might be helpful in determining how these two men came by their deaths?"

Barbara hesitated, looked away, made as if to speak, and then said in a very small voice, "Perhaps I ought to tell you one thing — only I don't know how to put it."

"Just go straight ahead."

"You might not believe me." She looked round at Capel, half addressing him. "Or you might laugh, or," back to Spearpoint, "be offended."

"I can promise we won't laugh; and policemen have no feelings as such."

"The point is: I want to keep slim."

The fat inspector kept a straight face

as he conceded that that was a laudable ideal.

"So I often go for long walks at night by myself. I need a lot of exercise. Tennis isn't enough."

"So you were out late on Saturday night?"

"Yes, I was. And I came along the lane behind the bach — a little before one. I didn't see anyone in the lane, or hear voices. There weren't any lights or noises in the bach."

"You didn't hear the shot which killed Mr. Boreman?"

"No, I didn't. The *kaivitis* were chanting on the beach, you know. I stopped and listened to them for a bit — after I'd passed the bach, of course. I was on my way home."

"What were they singing then?"

"Carols, mostly. *Once in Royal David's City. Hark! the Herald Angels Sing. Isa Lei,* later; and, as I was going up the hill afterwards, *Abide With Me.*"

"It might be useful to know what they were singing when the shot was fired.

Are you sure that was the order they sang them in?"

"I remember because the singing — impressed me. You see, I was feeling unhappy, after this quarrel with Jack — Mr. How. This singing did me good. I should say that after *Isa Lei* they sang *God Be With You Till We Meet Again.*" She threatened to become emotional, but managed to stave off her tears. "I expect you heard them in the distance. They were keeping time on the *lalis.* If I was near the beach and some distance from the bach when the shot was fired, the drumming might have drowned the noise of the shot."

"Quite. If I want you to sign a written statement, or to give evidence in Court, I'll let you know."

She got up and stuffed her handkerchief into her bag with a nervous gesture which again set Spearpoint wondering if she had told the full story.

"I — I hope you'll find out soon who killed him," she muttered; and walked out unsteadily.

Capel whistled. "Well, sir, she's a basket of oranges all right, isn't she? Did she do it?"

"How the hell should I know at this stage? The point is, she thinks someone may have seen her in the lane. We've got to find someone who did."

The telephone bell rang. It was Spearpoint's immediate superior, the Inspector-General in Suva.

"Here's a pointer for you, Spearo. A Mrs. Eliza Boreman landed from the *Duchess of Cleveland* from Samoa on Thursday. She walked straight out of the customs shed carrying a suitcase, and she hasn't been seen since. Any sign of her in Malua?"

"A woman whom no one now living admits to seeing was heard to ask How where Boreman was about ten last night. Sounded like a part-European. Could be her, sir?"

"Maybe. She looks Samoan — flat face, squashed nose, yellow complexion, straight black hair. Dresses European. Height, about five nine. Vital measurements given to me from guesswork as 50–48–60. And she has a great burn mark on the right side of her face, running from temple to jaw. Unique specimen, in fact."

"I'll find her if she's on this coast, sir."

"Meanwhile, I'm rounding up the taxi-*wallas* to find if any of them ran her round to Malua."

6

Louise Carwell's Story

NOT many of the white inhabitants of the Fiji Islands hope to be buried there. Even those who spend the long prime of their lives in the service of the Colonial Government, the trading firms or the sugar company — who lose all connection with the overseas lands of their birth and concentrate their interests into a few square miles of coral or volcanic soil in the wastes of the Pacific — still look forward to a few years of retirement in Herefordshire or Waipukurau, or by the beach at Coogee. But Death snatches as impatiently in the Paradise of the Pacific as he does Away, and many a surprised man fills a hurriedly-dug exile's grave under the waving palms within sound of the ever-rolling surf.

It would have disgusted as well as astonished Jack How and Joe Boreman had some bold fortune-teller prophesied that they would be buried side by side at the same funeral service; but neither would have been incredulous to be told that his funeral was to be the best-attended within living memory. Curiosity and the drama of their deaths drew many white and near-white citizens who would normally have preferred to spend their Sunday afternoon doting over a thriller; and drew also Indians and Chinese who would normally stay away from a Christian ceremony. The crowd was swollen by the complete native contingent who had been working on the timber ship; they regarded the ceremony as part of their holiday, and entered into the spirit of the business as few Europeans were sufficiently uninhibited to do. They wept unashamedly, and with such evident sincerity that many white men and most of the part-Europeans found their eyes uncomfortably moist.

Inspector Spearpoint was unwinking.

He bad spared time for the funeral only in the hope of gaining some clue to the solution of his problem. But no one (except the missing Harry Bennet) made himself conspicuous by his absence or his demeanour.

"We brought nothing into the world, and it is certain we can carry nothing out."

As he watched the native bearers lowering the coffins into the grave, Spearpoint wondered whether the two dead men were taking into the earth the secret of their deaths. Did either know how, and why, the other had died? Or would each have been astonished to learn of the death of the other? It was his job to find out; and the funeral gave him no help.

He arrived back at the Police Station as the sun was setting, and he paused for a moment. On the horizon silver grey islands turned suddenly to blood red, and the glow spread over the eastern sky also, and lit up the mountains in the interior, so that the Inspector seemed to be standing in a circle of fire. Then, in a flash, all the light went out, and he was in the dark with his problem.

Capel had arranged and summarised the reports from the constables who had been put on to gather information, and he suggested that three witnesses might be worth hearing, though he doubted if their evidence had more than negative value.

The sugar mill was working twenty four hours a day and seven days a week, for it was the crushing season; and there was a certain amount of coming and going all through Saturday night. The chance that someone had seen something vital was as great as the labour of finding that someone. The eagerness of the average man to put himself forward as a witness was apparently cancelled, in this case, by fear of being suspected of the crime if he admitted to having been anywhere near its scene.

It happened that during the darkness of Saturday night only two constables had been on patrol near R. L. & Co.

The first's beat took him along the coast road.

"Nothing twenty five, Inspector, Richmond, Lennox & Co., timber merchant, office. European man asleep on front porch. White trousers, dirty, crumpled shirt, dirty white shoes, white socks. Name, Henry Bennet. Occupation, labour foreman, Richmond, Lennox & Co. Snoring sleep. Mouth open. Breath too bad. Alcohol! Too bad, breath. Shook Henry Bennet. Result, nothing. Shook Henry Bennet two times. Shook Henry Bennet three times. Henry Bennet snoring sleep. Breath too bad. Patrol continued."

Knowing his man, Spearpoint refrained from asking questions. The report was complete. Questions would only provoke pained repetition.

The second constable followed the same route some three and a half hours later, about 4 a.m.

"Inspector Sahib, I march on coast road. I look right. I look left. I look forward. I look backward. All the time, I look right, I look left, I look backward,

107

I look forward. Four hours five minutes I look left. I see office, Richmond, Lennox and Company. I see no European man on porch. I see no European man on road. I see no European man on beach. The whole world, right, left, backward, forward, no man at all. This constable on patrol, the only man in world."

The third witness was both more important and less reliable than either of the constables. He was a very undersized, timid Indian labourer, who spoke no English. Everything he said, he repeated three times, in what seemed a pathetic (but hopeless) desire to be taken for a truthful man.

Translated, the interview ran thus:

You live in the Indian village, eh? — He did.

You worked at the mill last night, eh? — He did.

What time did you go home? — Two a.m.

Did you walk along the lane which leads from the mill to the Indian village? — The witness was volubly eager to insist that he had hurried along that most direct route, not diverging or pausing anywhere on the way.

Do you know a big kauri tree near the lamp-post in the lane? — He did. (This tree was some twenty yards on the mill side of the bach.)

The sergeant tells me that as you were passing that lamp post you saw a *sahib* standing by that tree? — It was the truth.

Are you sure it was a white man? — He was sure.

How tall was he? — He was not standing straight. He was crouching; but he was taller than the witness.

What did you think he was crouching for? — So that he should not be seen.

Why did you think that? — The witness could not explain his reasons, though he spoke for some minutes.

Did he see you? — He thought he had.

Do you think he knew that you saw him? — He was not sure. As soon as he saw the white man and decided he was trying not to be seen, the witness looked away and pretended he had seen nothing. He was afraid that if the *sahib* thought he had been observed, he would come and beat the witness for looking at him.

Did you see his face at all? — Most vehemently, no.

Would you recognise him if you saw him again? — Most vehemently, certainly not.

Was he wearing a hat? — No, but his head was black. (Harry Bennet was fair where he was not bald.)

Was he wearing a jacket? — Only shirt and trousers.

Was he carrying anything in his hand? — He could not remember seeing his hands. Then he corrected himself, and said that perhaps the man had a stick in his hand, or perhaps a gun. (But here, thought Spearpoint, he was saying what he thought his listener would like to hear.)

As soon as the Indian was dismissed, the sergeant ushered in the first witness who came voluntarily.

The ingredients in Louise Carwell's ancestry were precisely the same as those in Barbara Villiers', but the result looked very different. Louise's native forbears had presented her with her Melanesian features, her crinkly hair and her darkaline brown skin; her London ancestors had given her an ungainly and thin figure and a querulous voice. She had eyes like twin stars — small, yellow and close together.

So similar in ancestry and so different in appearance, the two girls had little in common beyond the fact that they lived in the same small community. Barbara had been educated mainly in New Zealand, and her chief hobby was lawn tennis. Louise had been taught to read and write and figure at the Mission School; she wrote beautifully and figured accurately; and she read avidly (and no doubt enviously) every piece of light fiction she could lay hands on. She lived in a large, rambling bungalow with a swarm of extraordinarily cheerful and philoprogenitive relations and semi-relations of diverse blood mixtures and skin colours — a frankly part-European world with no social contacts among either the full whites or the full blacks. Moving socially below Barbara, she felt herself a cut above because she was the cashier and Barbara was only a typist; but to the European community she aspired to join she was just the part-European girl in R. L. & Co.'s cash desk.

Her temper was unpredictable; her normal manner was submissive, but every now and then she would flare up like a Cockney at some fancied but unintended insult. Nature had entered this child for life's race with every handicap short of actual physical deformity.

Louise stalked into the Inspector's office with a half shy, half-defiant expression, which he had seen too often to regard as a clue to her present feelings — and motives.

Without preamble, she burst out, "Mr. Spearpoint, I've come to tell you who did those murders last night."

"Do you know who it was?"

"Yes, of course I know! Do you think I'd come to tell you if I didn't know?" All her Cockney ancestors spat out of her voice as she indignantly repudiated the slight.

"In that case, you'd better take a seat and tell us the whole story."

But Louise did not want to sit down. She came so close to the desk that she leaned against it and put her little eyes within a foot of Spearpoint's.

"It was that bitch Babs Villiers!"

"You saw her kill them?" he asked, unmoving.

"Of course I didn't see her kill them! Do you think I'd have let her kill them if I'd seen her doing it?"

"Then how do you know she killed them?"

"Because she was at the bach, and while she was there I heard shots and screams, and after that she came running past me along the lane."

"I see. Well, Miss Carwell, you'd better sit down calmly and tell us exactly what you saw and heard. Sub-Inspector Capel will write down what you say and then you can sign it. In Court, of course, you'll have to tell your story again and answer questions. You understand that, don't you?"

"Of course I do! I'm not stupid! What you mean is called cross-examination."

A hot temper lurked under Spearpoint's impassive manner, but he kept it down. "Yes. That's what I mean. Your story will have to stand up to cross-examination. Fire away!"

Half-an-hour occupied in indignant and discursive narrative by Louise, elucidatory questions by Spearpoint, and tactful editing by Capel, produced the following consecutive statement:

My name is Louise Carwell; aged 27; unmarried. I am cashier at Richmond, Lennox & Co.'s office at Malua. I live with my mother and other relations at a house at the end of the lane which leads from the sugar mill past the back of R. L. & Co.'s bach. My house is about a quarter of a mile from the bach. On Saturday night we had a birthday party for my sister Henrietta. About forty people were there and the guests did not go home until nearly midnight. After that I helped to put the young children to bed and to tidy up, and about one o'clock I went to the front gate to get a breath of fresh air. I had a headache. It was fairly dark, and I stood there for about ten minutes. The natives on the beach had been singing carols, but they had stopped for a while, though they began again later.

While I was standing there I heard a shot from the direction of the bach, then a scream. I am absolutely certain that I heard, first a shot and then a scream; and I am certain that these sounds came from the bach or quite near it. There are no other houses between my house and the bach. I can't remember if the natives had started to sing at the time of the shot. The only tune I remember hearing them sing was *Abide With Me.* But that was later. It did not occur to me to go and see what had happened at the bach because it was no business of mine what the men did there.

About five minutes after the shot Barbara Villiers came along the lane from the direction of the bach. She was going towards her home, which is at Althorp, about half-a-mile up the hill past my house. I could see her plainly in the light of the lamp standard at the road junction beyond my house, but she could not see me because I was standing under a tree. She was running when I first heard her footsteps, but when she came into the lamplight she was just walking very fast. She was panting and looked very distressed. I did not speak to her and she hurried on up the hill.

After standing there a little while longer and hearing nothing more from the bach I went to bed. It was not until the next morning that I heard what had happened at the bach.

(Signed) Louise Carwell.

A great deal of what Louise said was omitted from this statement, some of it despite her protests. Asked how she knew that Miss Villiers had been at the bach, she retorted, "Where else could she have been? She was always hanging round those fellows. She thinks that if she can trap one of them into marrying her, he'll take her to Australia and people will think she's real white — as if anyone would! One day one of them will put her in the family way, and serve her right!"

"Had she a particular friend at the bach?"

"She was out for any European she could get. But she hated Mr. Boreman. He wouldn't have anything to do with her. He could see what she was. He told her more than once to clear out and not keep hanging around. She was after Mr. How mostly. He didn't want her either, but he was too polite to be rude to her; and she made herself cheap and flattered him and told him the old, old story, but he wouldn't have anything to do with her, really."

"What about Mr. Anderton?"

"He'd be better than nothing, wouldn't

he? But you can't see him taking a black like her home to England as his wife, can you?"

Spearpoint allowed her to ramble on, in case some useful fact or clue emerged from the tangle of prejudice and wilful misunderstanding of the motives and actions of men and women. Louise asserted that she had supposed Barbara had murdered Mr. How because he had rejected her lewd advances, and then shot Mr. Boreman because he had caught her in the act. Either she did not know, or she blindly disregarded the fact that both men appeared to have been killed while peacefully asleep in bed.

Louise gratefully accepted Spearpoint's offer to drive her home, feeling it a deserved triumph to ride in a European's car, and not realising that his object was to see if her mother would corroborate her story.

Mrs. Carwell presented to the wondering world a small and elegant French head inherited from her father's side, and a tremendous Melanasian body inherited from her mother's side; by temperament she was almost entirely the South Sea Islander. In the normal way, she only stopped laughing in order to eat; but when some temporary misfortune overcame her, she wept fountains and bellowed sobs that could be heard as far away as the bach.

This evening, she was all smiles. "That good-for-nothing Jack How has got what was coming to him. Yes, sir!" she exulted, as soon as Spearpoint had firmly drawn her out of earshot of her daughter. "Now my little Louise will stop dreaming all day that he's going to marry her."

"Were they friendly?"

"One damn-sided friendship it was, Mr. Spearpoint. When he first came to Malua he took her to the pictures three-four times, and kissed her good-night on the back porch, keeping in practice like. Now every time he walked through the office she'd kneel down and lick the dust he'd trod in. If I've said to that silly girl once, I've said it ten hundred times,

'What d'you want to lick the dust he's trodden in for? A girl ought to have more self-respect.' But you can't talk sense into a young girl's head; and if I hadn't been as silly as she is, she'd never have been born. So I just let her carry on and make a damn fool of herself and say damn nothing. All I say to her is, she ought to stop stuffing herself with all these silly murder stories."

"Reads a lot of crime novels, does she?"

"Never reads anything else."

"Did Mr. How know what she felt about him?"

"Couldn't miss it, could he? If a girl kneels down and kisses the damn dust you've just trod in, a fellow can't help seeing she's barmy about him, can he?"

"Did he give her any encouragement?"

"Not since he took up with the girl Villiers. Of course, he'd slap Louise on the behind sometimes in passing, because he was a kind fellow, but it didn't mean a thing."

For the rest, Mrs. Carwell's evidence

(added to that of other people at the party, questioned later) was sufficient to establish the fact that Louise had been at home all the Saturday evening, and had gone out to the gate after the children had been put to bed. But no one knew how long she had been out there.

But much later that night, she was crying so noisily in bed that her mother went in to ask her what the matter was, and she said she had seen the girl Villiers hurrying home after visiting Jack How. It had not been until the milkman brought the news of the murders in the morning that she had mentioned the shot and the scream.

Spearpoint's route back took him through the sugar mill, and he was held up by a line of cane trucks on the narrow gauge railway. This was more fortunate than it appeared at the immediate moment of halting, for the sight of the mill gave him a useful idea.

The mill yard, drab enough by day, wore its usual eerie night aspect. The electric lighting, though more than adequate, was irregular, and created a patchwork of shifting shapes and shadows. Industrial activity seemed incongruous in a night intolerably sultry; and the volume of noise seemed out of all proportion to the number of human beings visible. There were drivers in the engines, clerks in the weighbridge offices, carpenters and engineers and labourers in the sheds; but hardly a man in the open. In the tall, paint-hungry iron buildings the machinery whirred and clanged; across the dusty, grassless marshalling yards, with their crisscross of tramlines, trundled the long lines of basket-like cane-trucks, led by fussy little George Stevenson engines, or molasses-snouted bullocks. It was uncanny to see so much activity without obvious direction.

Capel ventured, "You know, sir, there's something sinister about this place at night. I often wonder if there are murdered bodies hidden behind some of those piles of sugar sacks."

"We know that murders take place in quite ordinary surroundings, Capel; but

I'll grant you that the smell of a corpse might not be noticed here for months, though this isn't as nifty as some factories I've been in."

"I went into a tannery once, sir. That was an eye-opener. But a brewery would be best, wouldn't it? To be drowned in beer!"

Spearpoint did not respond to that. A thought had just struck him. "I'm glad you raised this, Capel. It might lead to something."

"Blimey!"

"I didn't mean that." The way being now clear, Spearpoint drove on — but to the mill office. There he consulted the night manager, and presently that obliging but sceptical man was leading the two policemen into the storage sheds and along the narrow alleyways between the mountains of bagged sugar awaiting shipment.

"Anyone could come into these alleyways," he conceded, "but who'd want to? And the watchmen make a complete round every night, you know."

Spearpoint did not answer, but presently he remarked quietly, "There's someone who came along here within the past twenty-four hours — but whether he walked or was carried, we shan't know until we examine him."

In the distance, half lying in the alleyway and half on a pile of empty sacks, was the figure of a man in dirty white shirt and trousers.

They broke into a run towards him.

It was Harry Bennet — but whether dead, drunk, or sleeping they could not immediately tell. There was blood on his shirt.

7

Harry Bennet's Story

HARRY BENNET was certainly not dead; but he was not exactly asleep; the smell hanging about him suggested that he was in a drunken drowse.

Spearpoint shook him without effect, and when they pulled him to his feet an empty brandy flask rolled from under him into the alleyway.

They dragged him into the open, and the air seemed to revive him a little. He muttered something unintelligible, and tried to break away from Capel's grasp. But this appeared to be a reflex action; when the attempt failed he relapsed into unconsciousness.

Efforts to revive him by slapping his face and dipping his head into a bucket of water had little effect; and

Spearpoint took the liberty of turning out his pockets. They yielded, among the usual oddments a man carries, one item which alarmed the Inspector: an empty aspirin bottle.

They bundled him into the car and drove along the coast to the hospital; there they left him medically in charge of the medical staff and legally under the surveillance of a police constable.

It was a very subdued and frightened Harry Bennet who, next morning, told the police the narrative which Capel presently shaped into the following:

My name is Harry Bennet, age 39, married, with five children and another expected any day. I am outside foreman for Richmond, Lennox & Co., timber merchants, of Malua; but on Saturday I was given a month's notice to leave that post, and I do not know where I shall find another job, as I am very well known in the Colony and I have been dismissed from several posts for habitual drunkenness. I am a very useful man with native and

Indian labour, and everyone says so; but I can't help drinking at times, and when I drink too much I am overcome. I wish I could get rid of this habit, but drinking is my only pleasure in life; sometimes I think that without liquor my life would not be worth living.

It was Joe Boreman who had me dismissed on Saturday. He said I was asleep all Thursday afternoon when I ought to have been tallying timber off the *Frances Teresa,* but that isn't true. I only dozed off for about ten minutes, and only three lorry loads left the ship without my counting them. And the boss-boy at the wharf was very reliable. But Joe Boreman told Mr. Tilson that if I wasn't sacked, he'd chuck up his job, so Mr. Tilson gave me a month's notice.

In the evening, I went to Jack How's room at R. L. & Co's bach, where he had a number of his cobbers. I regret to say I tried to drown my sorrows there, and I drowned them too deep. I remember very little about the early part of the evening. We sat round and yarned and drank beer and played darts and sang a few songs, and Jack played his gramophone. I remember Anderton coming in and saying he was going down to the hotel. I don't remember a woman asking for Boreman. I remember I told the other fellows about my dismissal, and I think I began to get very hot and silly, and it may be that I threatened to murder Boreman, but I don't remember exactly what I said. All this is very confused in my mind, but I do have a vague idea that I did try to go into Boreman's room and hit him over the head with a bottle. I think the other fellows took me along to Boreman's room and showed me he wasn't there. After that, I don't remember any more until I woke up and found myself on R. L. & Co.'s front porch.

Everything was quiet and I had the usual headache and my mouth was dry and felt like a dog's breakfast. There was a bit of a breeze from the sea and the night was dark. I was stiff all over; I didn't know what the time was, but I thought I'd better go home.

When I got up I found I couldn't walk straight, because I had cramp in both legs, and I knew I couldn't walk all the way to my house at Althorp in the state I was in. First I thought I'd better lie down and go to sleep again. But then I decided to go up to the bach and hit Joe Boreman in the face with a bottle. So I made my way up to the bach. I stumbled once or twice, and once I fell over a root. But I managed to pull myself on to the veranda of the bach and found an empty bottle just by the entrance to Jack How's room, and I went along to Boreman's room. I had to hold on to things to keep from falling over, and I worked my way round between his bed and the chest-of-drawers, and I kicked something on the floor. I didn't know what it was.

I began to pull at the mosquito-net, and then I noticed that I couldn't hear Boreman breathing, and the thought struck me that he was awake and knew I was there and was holding his breath so that as soon as I put my head and shoulders under the net to bash him with the dead marine, he'd grab me by the throat and throttle me. So I stood there for longer than a man could hold his breath and I couldn't hear a thing and I began to feel frightened. So before I'd got the net properly pulled out, I took my torch in my left hand and switched it on and pointed it at the pillow. And when I saw what was there, I screamed and dropped the torch and fell forward on to the bed.

For what I saw was Joe Boreman with his eyes open and his teeth bared in a snarl, and blood on the pillow; and that's where I must have got the blood on my shirt — when I fell forward on to him outside the net. Well, I didn't know what to do then, because I wasn't sure whether I was drunk or seeing things; so I picked up the torch, which was caught in the net, and switched it off and went back and stood in the doorway and pinched myself to see if I was awake or dreaming. I don't know how long I stood there, but it seemed like hours.

I was shivering with fright in case Joe Boreman leapt out of bed with his face all bloody and came after me; and I couldn't tear myself away either.

In the end, I managed to pluck up the courage to go back into the room and turn the torch on him again; and I could see he was dead all right. I could see he'd been shot through the head and that what I'd kicked on the floor had been the revolver. So I tucked the net in and stood the bottle on the floor, and thought I'd better go along to Jack How's room and see if I could find some brandy there. I remembered that Jack How had said he had a flask of brandy. It never occurred to me at that time to wake Jack How up and tell him what had happened. I did think of going to the police, but I was afraid you'd think I'd shot Boreman and I didn't dare. I think I was sobered up by this time, because I hadn't got the cramp any more, and I could think clearly in a way, and I can remember what I was thinking. But if I'd been stone cold sober I'd have gone to the police. But all I could think was that I'd been threatening to murder Boreman and here he was shot and I'd been wandering about the compound.

One thing I ought to say is that I noticed Boreman was wearing his day shirt, and that the pockets were buttoned, and one was bulging. I thought at the time that it was his cigarette-case, because I'd forgotten that he'd put the *Kaivitis'* wages in that pocket at lunch-time, when they'd asked him to hold the money until Sunday. I didn't take that money, I swear I didn't. All I took from Boreman's room was a bottle of aspirin which was on the chest-of-drawers.

So I went along to Jack How's room, and I flashed my torch on to the cupboard, and the key was in the lock, so I opened the door and took out the brandy. And then it struck me that Jack How wasn't breathing either, and everything seemed unnaturally still. And I stood there in agony, wondering if he'd been shot, too; or if he was awake and knew I was stealing his brandy. So presently I put the flask down and went over to the bed, and sure enough there was someone in it; but even when I was quite close I couldn't hear his breathing. So it took me a long time to turn the torch on to him, and it gave me another shock when I saw him. Because he was dead, too. His eyes and mouth were open and his tongue stuck out. It gave me a terrible shock to see him like that, when I'd been drinking with him only a few hours before.

I picked up the brandy flask and ran out of the place as fast as I could and along the lane towards the mill. I must have been pretty well sobered up by these shocks, because although I made record time out of the bach I didn't trip up at all.

I can't explain why I went towards the mill instead of in the opposite direction, to my home. Perhaps it was the mill was the nearest place where I should find living people. I can tell you, I was dead scared by that time, and when a man's in that state he doesn't act by reason.

When I got to the mill and saw everything was going on as usual, I bucked up a bit; and when I saw an Indian in the distance coming towards me, I thought I'd better find a quiet place to sit down and think out what to do. I was sober enough to realise that I'd better not be seen coming from the direction of the bach. So I skirted round the back of the warehouse and found a quiet pozzy in one of the sugar stores. Everything was so normal that I began to wonder whether what I'd seen at the bach was real or not. Of course, I had to take some brandy to help me to think, and then, with the brandy inside me on top of the beer, I decided that the best thing to do would be to swallow all the aspirins and wash them down with a long swig of the brandy, and so finish myself for good and all, and that would be good riddance to bad rubbish, because I had brought all this trouble and misery on my wife and myself because I couldn't keep off the booze. What I thought about my wife and kids was that it would be better for them if I killed myself than if I was hanged for murder, because although I didn't kill Joe Boreman and Jack How, and don't know who did, it would look as if I did, and no one would believe me if I said I didn't.

But I was all confused, because in the clamour and stink of the mill everything seemed O.K., and I could hardly believe that Joe Boreman and Jack How were lying dead in the bach. Still, I choked down the aspirin and swallowed the brandy, but I couldn't get it all down at one gulp, because I began to cough and I had to stop, because though I wanted to die, when it came to it, I didn't want to die choking and gasping like that; all I wanted was to go to sleep and not wake up. And it seemed such a waste of brandy to pour it down and not taste it.

Well, I did go to sleep all right, but I woke up this morning in hospital here, and I don't know what the hell will become of me now. I swear to God that I did not murder Joe Boreman or Jack How, and that I haven't the slightest idea who did murder them. They were dead when I found them, and that's the truth.

(Signed) Harry Bennet.

He signed the statement with an almost steady hand, and then looked up anxiously at the Inspector.

"Are you going to arrest me? I swear I didn't do it. I'd kiss my thumb on the Bible it's all true, this paper."

"What I'm going to do, Mr. Bennet, is to arrest you for stealing one bottle of aspirin from the late Mr. Boreman and one flask of brandy from the late Mr. How. I propose to keep a guard over you while you are in hospital, which I understand will be for at least another twenty-four hours. After that — wait and see."

Driving away from the hospital, Spearpoint turned into the lane behind the bach. At the far end, where it joined the main road to Althorp, Ba and Lautoka, stood the long, low building of Kanhai's Indian laundry.

He pulled up and, followed by Capel, pushed his way under a line of flapping shirts and trousers to the *dhobi's* station. August Bank Holiday was no holiday for washermen.

"You and your *wallas* were working as usual late on Saturday night, eh?"

"Yes, *sahib,* until the stone end of Saturday."

"Did you see any Europeans pass along the lane between, about, ten and midnight?"

Kanhai considered, called his boys into a huddle and consulted them. From their excited jabbering, so fast and with so many voices at once that neither of the Hindi-diploma'd policemen could follow the conversation fully, there emerged agreement that a man had walked along towards the bach about eleven o'clock. They provided a sufficient description to identify the man beyond doubt.

One of the more dim-witted *dhobi-wallas* asserted that he had noticed a big woman in European clothes walking along the lane, but, further questioned, he could not be sure whether this had been Friday or Saturday, or what the time had been, or which way she had been going.

At the hotel, Spearpoint demanded of the landlord a list of the revellers who had been celebrating on the beach, and particularly of those whose voices had been heard right up to the end. He sorted the list into two parts and gave one part to Capel.

"Dig out all these chaps and ask them if they saw anyone round at the back of the hotel late Saturday night. You know who I think may have been there, but don't put the thought into anyone's mind."

"*Eo, saka.* Can do."

Spearpoint himself took the rest of the list. It was a frustrating business, but not unfruitful. He arrived back at the office to find a message from Suva that so far there had been no trace of Mrs. Boreman. The taxi drivers all denied taking her for any journey, and produced their log-books to prove it. Nor had she travelled on the Indian-run bus, patronised almost entirely by the darker-skinned sections of the population, which did the round journey between Suva and Malua every day.

Then Capel returned with sufficient evidence to justify calling to the police station a man who, if not the murderer, certainly had a great deal to explain.

8

Anderton's Second Story

THE nervous young man came in looking anxious; had he been jaunty and self-confident he would have made a more unfavourable impression.

"Now, Mr. Anderton," Spearpoint began formally, "please take a seat. The more we look into this horrible business at the bach, the more mysterious it becomes. You remember you suggested those two fellows might have killed each other?"

"It — it seems the only possible explanation."

"It is certainly impossible."

Anderton looked doubtfully at the Inspector, and then away; as Spearpoint regarded him without saying anything, he asked nervously, "Are you going to tell me why?"

"That's one of the reasons why I

asked you here. That booby-trap was an obvious and clumsy fake. Firstly, the revolver can't be jammed in the drawer in such a way as to make it possible for the cord to pull the trigger back; secondly, the cord was a good deal too long to be stretched taut between the bed-post and the drawer; thirdly, if it had been stretched taut it would have raised the pillow suspiciously high at the revolver end, and it would also have had to loop up the mosquito-net; fourthly, if the jerk on the trigger was strong enough to pull the revolver on to the floor, the murderer could not have been sure the bullet would have hit its mark; and finally, Boreman was shot from less than a foot away, whereas the drawer was nearly a yard from his head. And even if the booby-trap could have been rigged up to overcome all these practical difficulties, whoever rigged it up could not be certain that Boreman wouldn't turn on the light and discover the trap, or that he wouldn't set off the revolver with some other portion of his anatomy before putting his head on the pillow. It is as certain as anything can be that Boreman was shot after he had gone to bed by someone who fired the revolver at close range and then rigged up the fake booby-trap — and probably also stole the hundred and forty-seven pounds from Boreman's shirt pocket."

Anderton stared at the floor in silence for a minute or so; then he suggested, "How could have done all that, couldn't he?"

"Not after Boreman had suffocated him. If How killed Boreman, someone else killed How. Conversely, if Boreman killed How, then someone else killed Boreman."

"Y-yes, I-I see that."

"Besides, if Boreman smothered How, would he have gone calmly to bed? If How shot Boreman, would he have gone calmly to bed? How couldn't reasonably have pretended that he was asleep and didn't hear the shot. Nor would he have faked the booby-trap to make believe Boreman had shot himself, because everyone who knew Boreman would know that if he'd wanted to commit suicide he'd have put the revolver to his head and pulled the trigger."

"You mean that neither killed the other?"

"I do. What do you think?"

Anderton frowned. "What you say seems right enough; but doesn't it mean that How must have been killed first — otherwise he'd have heard the shot and not gone to bed?"

"That's a fair point. But, now, perhaps you can tell us what really happened?"

Anderton started, and then coloured. "I don't know what you mean," he muttered.

Spearpoint did not answer that. He stared grimly at the young man, who looked everywhere but at the Inspector. At last, however, his gaze happened to meet Spearpoint's, and he began to cough and hid his face in his handkerchief.

Spearpoint waited until he had finished coughing and was obliged to uncover his face.

"When a witness hides something from the police, the police become very interested to find out what he is hiding and why. I must warn you that anything you say will be taken down and may be used in evidence. And you're entitled to refuse to say anything at all. But before I try some other means of finding out the truth, I am giving you the chance to add to and correct the story you told me yesterday morning."

Anderton looked up quickly, and then down again, muttering, "There's nothing to add."

"There is, you know. I want the full truth."

"But I've told you the truth," he protested.

"It was not true that you slept soundly all night at the hotel. There were a dozen fellows with a ukulele and a steel guitar and a drum kicking up hell until half past one just on the other side of the hotel. I heard them in my house a quarter of a mile away. And there was a fist fight with the rest cheering the fighters on, and Joe Battrum shouting the odds. You couldn't have slept through that."

"I heard a bit of noise," Anderton conceded, "but they didn't keep me awake long."

"No. You weren't there. Two of those chaps, walking back to their quarters, when the party broke up just before two, saw a man slinking up the staircase leading to your room."

"You can't prove that was me," Anderton challenged, desperately. "It could have been a night prowler."

"I can prove that you walked past Kanhai's laundry in the direction of the bach shortly after eleven o'clock on Saturday night. Three *dhobi-wallas* saw you."

This shook Anderton, and he ceased his denials.

Spearpoint went on, remorseless. "They are prepared to swear to your identity. Just after eleven. Walking towards the bach. Two other men saw someone going up the staircase to your room about one forty-five. Boreman was shot about ten past one. How was smothered about the same time. You'd better come clean, hadn't you?"

"I swear I didn't have anything to do with their being murdered, or with fixing up the booby-trap. I didn't set foot in the bach from the time I told How I was going to the hotel for the night until I went back for breakfast on Sunday morning."

"That's as maybe. I'll give you a choice. Either you tell your story — and the truth, mind you, this time — and let Sub-Inspector Capel take it down for you to sign; or else I shall arrest you on the charge of being concerned in the murder of your two bachmates, and you can tell your story in Court. If you're innocent, your only chance of walking out of here a free man is to cooperate with the police."

The unhappy young man shifted uneasily in his seat, and asked, "Can I have time to think about that?"

"I can't give you time to think up another story. You can have two minutes to decide whether to tell the truth or whether to be arrested."

Spearpoint took off his watch, and put it on the desk.

Less than a minute passed before Anderton broke.

"After all, I didn't do anything wrong, so I may as well tell you everything. The fact is, I've been trying to keep Miss Villiers' name out of the business. But you don't leave me much option do you?"

"That is entirely the wrong way to look at the matter. It is the duty of every citizen who becomes aware of a crime to tell the police everything he knows — and at once — without attempting to shield anyone."

"All right." Anderton's story, partly given in direct narrative and partly in answer to Spearpoint's questioning, was tactfully edited by Capel into the following statement:

My name is Harry Anderton, twenty-four years old, unmarried. I have been in the Colony for two years, employed by Marryam & Cutt, Ltd., at Suva and Lautoka until five weeks ago, when I left that firm and came to Malua to take up a post as clerk in the office of Richmond, Lennox & Co. As soon as I joined this firm, I fell in love with Miss Villiers, the shorthand-typist in the office. She did not seem to be attracted to me, and I was very unhappy in consequence. I have never been in love properly before, and I was crazy about her, and wretched because she did not reciprocate my feelings. I soon observed that she was very friendly with Mr. How, the motor mechanic, who lived in the firm's bachelor quarters with me. They went out together in the evenings; and I could tell by the way she looked at him when he came into the office that she was very fond of him. I could not understand why so nice a girl could be so fascinated by such a rotter. He used to speak most disrespectfully — even obscenely — about her and about other girls in my hearing, and I thought it was a damnable shame that such a pure and attractive girl should fall for a man who did not value her and respect and appreciate her.

(Anderton broke off to say in parenthesis, "You know what he called her once at the bach? He said she was his *saisai matairua.* I don't know what that means, but I know it's a filthy thing to say of a girl."

The two policemen laughed.

Spearpoint explained, "It's not really you know."

Capel ventured, "I should think — wouldn't you, sir? — that it's probably pretty accurate."

Anderton flushed, and protested, almost fiercely, "You can laugh, but I'm sure she's a nice girl."

"I dare say she is," Spearpoint explained. "If you come to a country, you ought to be careful to learn the meaning of any native words you use. *Saisai matairua* means a two pronged spear; but in the sense in which How used it, it means that she was well developed above the waist. Obviously she is, even if you've never seen her in a bathing costume."

"Well, I don't think that's a nice thing to say about a girl.")

How and Boreman never spoke to each other, but they used to talk at each other through me. One day Boreman said to me that the typist was no better than she ought to be. How retorted that she was just about as good as a girl could be — only he meant it as an insult, I think. And when I said that I thought they were both wrong, and that she was a thoroughly nice and innocent girl, Boreman jeered and said that before I came to the bach she often used to creep into How's room at night, and that my coming had driven them off into the bushes. How laughed and said that Boreman was jealous because no girl would ever let him drag her into the bushes. And later on, after How had gone, Boreman said that if I'd clear out one night and come back unexpectedly, I'd catch her in How's bed.

I knew that would be a mean thing to do, but I was desperately in love with Miss Villiers, and I was jealous of the way How spoke about her, and I wanted to prove to myself that Boreman was wrong. On Saturday morning, How came into the office and told my chief, Mr. Maitland, that he was having a party that evening, but it would be over by midnight, so it wouldn't keep the compound awake till all hours. The bach is a long way from Mr. Maitland's house, and I thought that How's real purpose might be to let Miss Villiers know that the coast would be clear by twelve. So I decided to use the party as an excuse for clearing out for a night so that I could test my suspicions. I went down to the hotel and booked a room and about a quarter past eleven I came out, locked the door behind me, and went down the outside stairs. It was a dark night and I kept in the shadows, and I thought I reached R. L. & Co.'s compound without being seen. I hid behind the banana clumps where I could see into the compound on How's side of the bach.

I couldn't hear what they were saying in How's room, but I could hear the voices and recognise who the men were. A few minutes before twelve a woman came into the compound from the direction of Althorp, where Miss Villiers lives. I couldn't see her properly, because it was a dark night, and I was keeping well back. But she was tall, and I caught the scent Miss Villiers uses, so I was sure it was her. She stood under a tree, between me and the bach, and waited, quite still. If it was not for her scent, which came to me clearly, and nearly drove me mad with love and jealousy, I should not have been certain she was there.

I felt pretty sick at her coming, and I had half a mind to go out and confront her, but I had no right to do that, for I had no claim on her at all, only the fact that I was in love with her. And she didn't know that, and wasn't interested in me, so I couldn't reprove her for running after that rotter How. I ought to have gone away then, for I had seen all I needed to know, but I couldn't tear myself away. I wanted to know the worst.

It was twisting the dagger in my wound. And so the two of us stood there, almost within touching distance. I'm sure she didn't know I was there.

Another thing that got me worked up was that the natives on the beach were chanting and drumming — a steady, maddening throb. It got on my nerves, and what with that and the scent and my love and jealousy, I was half mad. But I just had to stand there and wait, with everything in a turmoil inside me.

Presently, the party broke up. They were very noisy about it. Four of them carried Harry Bennet by arms and legs, with a lot of silly laughter and shouting and joking, through the compound towards the coast road. When they'd gone, and all was quiet at the bach, Miss Villiers went forward and tapped on the window of How's room, and he came out to her, and they stood at the side of the veranda, right in front of where I was, and put their arms round each other and stood there kissing. Although it was such a dark night, they showed up against the white paint, so I was sure it was them.

Besides, I could recognise their voices, though I couldn't catch all they said, because they were whispering. But I did hear How say something about taking her clothes off; and after he'd said that, they went round to the front of the bach, and I could hear their footsteps on the veranda and in his room. She was walking in front of him and he was close behind her with his arms round her and her whole attitude suggested that she went very willingly.

And I felt absolutely sick and disgusted.

Everything was silent in the bach, but the natives were banging away on the beach, and something seemed to be throbbing in my brain, and I nearly decided to rush into How's room and turn the light on and taunt them. But I didn't. I felt sick and I didn't see any point in staying, but I couldn't tear myself away. I walked a little way towards the hotel, and sat down behind a tree and wondered what to do. After some time — it may have been as much as half an hour — I went back to about fifty yards from the bach. There was a torch being moved round in How's room, but then it went out, and I couldn't hear anything from the bach. The natives were not drumming but they were singing *Isa Lei.* It was about one o'clock, and I was feeling tired and stiff with standing still. So I started back to the hotel. It was a good deal lighter then.

And then suddenly, without any warning at all, there was this bang — the revolver shot. Just that, and then silence. It scared me for a minute — the fact that there was no more noise afterwards. The birds in the trees began twittering, and one big bird flapped its wings and flew away. I walked back towards the bach, but everything was silent there; and I didn't dare go into the compound, so I just hesitated, some fifty yards along the lane, waiting for I don't know what. Frankly, I was too frightened to go either way; you see, I had been in such a turmoil that this sudden shot was more than I could stand. I knew that Jack How had a gun, because he'd shot that pigeon with it, and I wondered if he'd shot Miss Villiers, or if she had shot him, or herself or what. And the silence was absolutely unnerving. After a long time — I don't know how long, but it may have been as much as a quarter of an hour, or it may have been less, I heard footsteps, and a woman came past the side of the bach — just a dark figure against the white paint — and hurried into the lane. I could hear her running along the lane, away from me, towards Althorp, where Miss Villiers lives.

I couldn't see this woman at all clearly, because there were bushes in the way and I was at least fifty yards from the bach, but I took it for granted that it was Miss Villiers, because I had seen her go into the bach and she was running off in the direction of her home.

After that, I went back to the hotel. I didn't meet anyone on the way, and I thought I got back without being seen. It was twenty to two when I looked at my watch in my room, so I suppose the shot must have been fired about a quarter past one.

I didn't tell all this to the police when they first questioned me, because I was afraid it would compromise Miss Villiers. Not only had I seen her in the bach with How; but in the morning Boreman had pinched her in the office and she had slapped his face and told Mr. Maitland she'd murder Boreman if he didn't stop pestering her. So things looked black against her, but I don't believe she is a murderer, and, even if she was, I would not like to be a witness against her. I don't know what to think happened in the bach on Saturday night.

(Signed) Harry Anderton

Considering this document (which Anderton had signed with an obviously-practised right hand), Spearpoint asked, "On Sunday morning you were wearing a khaki shirt and brown trousers, and dark shoes. Was that the rig-out you were wearing the night before?"

"Yes. I thought I'd be less likely to be noticed than if I wore whites."

"But even on a dark night your face and hands would show up."

"Well, I thought of that. When I was hiding in the bushes, I put on a cap and gloves and tied a dark handkerchief round the lower part of my face."

"Can you produce the handkerchief?"

"I'm afraid I can't. I think I must have dropped it when I sort of panicked when the gun went off and I forgot all about it until next morning."

"But you're sure you dropped it in the lane?"

"Yes. At least, I don't see where else I could have dropped it."

Spearpoint took a blue silk handkerchief from the drawer of his desk and held it up. "Can this be it?"

Anderton gulped. He was badly shaken.

"It could be," he admitted, "Where did you find it?"

"In the open drawer of Boreman's chest-of-drawers. It had apparently been used to hold the revolver so that there should be no fingermarks on it."

Anderton stared, and then suggested.

"Whoever fired the gun must have picked it up after I dropped it."

"But you said you dropped it when the shot was fired."

"May I see it?" Anderton held out his hand, and Spearpoint gave him the handkerchief.

Anderton examined it carefully, and then sniffed at it. He looked up anxiously. "It's not mine," he said, with a mixture of relief and reluctance. "It's scented."

"So what?"

"Well, it can't be mine, can it? I don't use scent. You say you found it in Boreman's drawer?"

"Yes. You're not suggesting he used scent?"

Anderton suddenly leapt to his feet and went stumping about the office. *"Damn and blast!"* he shouted. *"Damn and blast!"* He made the oath sound more shocking than any obscenity Joe Boreman ever uttered. "I wish to heaven I'd never meddled in the business!"

Spearpoint waited until he had calmed down, and then asked, "What have you to say now?"

Anderton came to him and flung the handkerchief down on his desk, "I suppose I must tell you," he said, slowly. "Though I hate to say it. But Miss Villiers had a blue silk handkerchief just like mine — like this. And this is the scent she uses."

9

Barbara's Second Story

SPEARPOINT was feeling a trifle impatient at the young lover's expressions of emotion. He said briskly, "If you had told this story at first, well and good. But you told a series of lies yesterday, and while I don't say that I disbelieve all that you have now said, I must point out that this is not entirely satisfactory. I must ask you to wait here while I make some further enquiries."

Anderton looked surprised and disconcerted. Then he flushed, and asked, shakily, "You mean I'm under arrest?"

"Not at all, I'm asking for your help. I'm asking you to wait here in case I want to ask you anything more."

"If that's what you want — . Of course, I want to get the thing cleared up, too."

But his words were more cooperative than his manner. When he had been settled with a jig-saw puzzle in a room from which he could not see who came into the police station, Spearpoint remarked to Capel, "There may be some truth in that young man's story. Nothing upsets a liar more than to be disbelieved when he's telling the truth."

"If he's told all the truth, sir, I'll eat my hat."

Barbara Villiers came in with her natural dignity, but there was alarm in her eyes.

"Sit down, Miss Villiers. First, I think you may like to see this." Spearpoint handed her a cable which had arrived a few minutes earlier from the Melbourne police.

She read it gravely and handed it back without a word.

"He never told you that, did he?"

She made a gesture, pathetic in its hopelessness, which could be interpreted either way. Her eyes were swimming in tears. It was possible she could not trust herself to speak.

Spearpoint hardened his heart. "I am sorry to have to say this to you, Miss Villiers, but I have witnesses who allege that you were in the bach with Mr. How about midnight on Saturday."

She began to sob without restraint.

Policemen cannot be deflected from their duty by a lovely woman's tears, and they waited grimly until she recovered. It was impossible to tell whether her emotion was real or simulated. But presently she wiped her eyes, and held her head up, and indicated that she was prepared to submit to Spearpoint's questioning.

"Are you going to tell us the truth now, or would you prefer to consult a solicitor?"

"I'm very sorry. I know I ought to have told you all the story yesterday. I was silly, but I was so upset, I didn't know what to say. And I wanted time to think. It was all such a nightmare! But I'll tell you everything now. I've slept on it, and decided that that's the only thing."

Spearpoint wondered if she would have come to him with this promise if she had not been sent for. He cautioned her formally. She replied that she didn't care, they could make what use they liked of her confession.

"But there's one point," she added, in some confusion. "I'm not sure I want that told — yet."

"You tell your story, Miss Villiers, and we'll discuss later what parts of it need not be used in Court."

Her narrative was partly incoherent. It was repetitive, and some parts of it were brought out by questioning. Her successive emotions were implied rather than expressed; but this was the story she tried to tell.

When the merriment of the departing revellers was merely a babble in the distance, Barbara glided from the shelter of the trees and went to Jack How's window. She could not see in, but the light was on, and she could hear movements inside the room. She gave the double tap which was her signal, and waited anxiously for his answer. Would he be too full of beer to be kind?

After three or four interminable minutes, she tapped again.

The light went out, and then he was suddenly upon her. He wore nothing but pyjama trousers and canvas shoes, and his body gleamed white in the darkness. He seized her tight in his arms, holding her mouth in a beery kiss.

The natives on the beach were beating their *lalis* in a steady rhythm which set her pulses throbbing, and she responded eagerly to his embrace, though the cooler part of her brain struggled to retain control.

When he wrenched his lips away, and she drew a relieved breath, he whispered urgently, "Come inside, loloma, and take all those clothes off. The Boy Friend's gone down to the pub to sleep in his dream world, and Boreman is riding his piebald mare. So it's all ours tonight."

She held back, "No. I want to talk to you, darling."

"Can't talk now. This is the time and the place for action, my *saisai matairua.*" He kissed her again.

She responded to his kiss, but when he broke off she repeated, "I must talk to you."

"Why the hell were women given tongues? They'd be much better without. Tell me everything tomorrow."

"No, darling: now. I must!"

"You must not, ducky! Look! meet me in church and you can talk to me all through prayers."

"Don't be silly, Jack. Listen a minute."

His only response was to fasten her once more in his sweaty embrace and silence her in a long kiss; and in spite of herself, she felt her resolution melting.

"Now," he whispered, when their mouths separated again, "into my room and off with those clothes — shoot!"

He twisted her round, so that her back was to him, and grasped her arms and made her march forward thus a prisoner. She could have fought him off, but she went obediently. She had determined that they must talk things out under cover of darkness, and tonight, but her whole being throbbed with desire for him.

As soon as they were in his room, he pulled her round again and seized her so tightly that he seemed to have half-a-dozen arms. And he began to fumble with the button at the back of her dress. His ardour almost overcame her, but the drumming on the beach was fainter now, and she summoned up all her powers of resistance.

She struggled, and because she was as strong as he was, and he did not realise her intention, she managed to bend an elbow up and get a hand under his chin and push his face away.

He was surprised at her vigour.

"Steady on, *marama*. Do you want to break my ruddy neck?"

She had his face between her two hands now and held him off. Her wrists were strong with tennis and hockey.

167

"I want you to listen to me," she whispered desperately. "You must listen. I must tell you. I'm going to have a baby."

He tugged himself right away at that, and said flatly, "I don't believe it."

"You've got to believe it. It's true."

"Nonsense."

"It isn't nonsense. It's certain."

"Are you sure?" he asked, stupidly.

"Haven't I told you I'm sure?"

"How long have you been like that?"

"Three months." She made to caress him, but he drew back.

"Have you been to a doctor — or anyone?"

"Not yet." She added, "But there's no doubt about it."

"Have you told anyone?"

"Of course not. I'd tell you first."

He said nothing for a minute, and again resisted her attempt to caress him. Then, explosively, "You're a damned fool, aren't you?"

She was stung, and retorted, "You're making me feel I was — but not the way you mean?"

"Why not?"

"That way it's you that was the damned fool. I warned you this might happen, and you just laughed and said you'd take the risk."

"You said *you'd* take the risk."

"I didn't say I wanted to. What I said was that it would be me that would be taking it."

"You were a damned fool not to do something about it afterwards."

"I did, when I could. But it must have been too late."

He turned away, muttering, "That's your story!"

She began to cry at the unkindness of that, holding out her arms to him, but he avoided her; and they stood in unspeaking dismay, as so many couples in their predicament have stood since the world began, each in their lonely agony, and further apart than they had ever been.

She pleaded, "You'll have to let me tell people now."

He deliberately misunderstood her, and asked brutally, "What? That you're in the family way?"

"You know what I mean!"

He became nasty. "You'd better be careful what you say. I don't believe it happened that week-end. You're just using that."

"What do you mean?"

"How do I know it's my kid?"

She swallowed hard, and answered submissively, "Darling, you've been drinking. I don't think you know what you're saying."

He was so self-righteously and drunkenly angry that he forgot to keep his voice down, "Who's the father? That's what I'm asking."

She smacked him right and left across the cheeks with such fury that he shook sideways, and he had to cling to her to keep his balance; and when Joe Boreman tiptoed along the veranda and switched on the light a few seconds later he caught them wrestling absurdly in the middle of the room.

"What the bloody hell's going on here?"

They broke apart and How ordered him to switch off the light and get to hell out of it.

Boreman leant against the door-post, protecting the light switch, and pointed out that this was a respectable bloody bach, or that at least it ought to be, and he was determined to see fair play.

"What are the rules in this bloody fight? Who undresses who? I'll umpire it."

Barbara, having hastily buttoned up her dress, sank down on a chair and began wiping her eyes.

Boreman glared at her with contempt. "So you're in the family way at last, are you?"

She did not deign to answer that.

"You're trying to kid him he's the father, are you?"

"Yes, he is!"

"How the hell can you possibly know?"

How cut in with, "That's no business of yours."

"He's dead right there," Boreman confided to the bed. "I wouldn't use her for practice."

Barbara retorted, "There isn't a decent girl in the Colony who'd give you the practice."

"We're not talking about decent girls."

She turned to How. "Are you going to stand by and listen to this cheap larrikin insulting your wife?"

"His what?"

She stood up, and took How's reluctant arm, proclaiming "Jack and I were married six months ago!"

"That's what you think!"

"We were married in Sydney — properly, before witnesses."

Boreman laughed contemptuously.

"So perhaps, Mr. Boreman, you would be so good as to return to your room and leave me alone with my husband."

"Your husband!" Boreman did not stir. "Does he admit he married you in Sydney last March?"

"He can't deny it."

"He can, you know!" Boreman sat

172

down and crossed his legs, and gave her a pitying stare. "I accept your word, *Miss* Villiers, that you went through a ceremony of so-called matrimony with this lilywhite louse in bloody Sydney last March. But I don't expect he told you that he had, and still has, a wife and two snotty-nosed kids in bloody Melbourne, did he?"

Barbara found herself unable to stand, and she sat down, saying faintly that she did not believe it; but Jack How's face was sufficient corroboration.

He turned to Boreman and swore obscenely at him, telling him to get out.

Boreman ignored him completely. "It's a small bloody world, Miss Villiers," he went on, with relish. "I've a married sister in Melbourne. My last leave, I toddled over to pay my ruddy respects, and my sister told me she had a friend who had a friend who knew a woman whose husband was in Malua — a Mrs. How. So I pricked up my bloody ears at that, and I made a few ruddy enquiries, and I took a corkeye at this Mrs. Jack How, and her two face-ached bloody kids, and I can assure you, Miss Villiers, that they're the dead spits of their dad. Spits is the right bloody word."

"*Get out!* — Tell him to get to hell out of it, Barbara!"

Boreman went on cheerfully, "So, Miss Villiers — *Miss* Mother-to-be Villiers, I should say, if he dragged you by the back hair up the aisle in Sydney, he's a bloody bigamist, and if he ever goes back to Aussie, he'll find himself cooling his ardour in the ruddy jug. And they won't let him take that ruddy knocking rug in there, believe you me! And whether you think he married you or not, and whether he goes to clink or not, your kid will be a bloody half-caste bastard, and you can stick your bloody tar-brush nose in the air and think that one out!"

She had been trying to get How to look her in the face, but he would not; and now she sat with her hands covering her eyes, not weeping, but wishing desperately that she could weep.

Boreman got to his feet, and stood over her, jeering. "And for all we know, Miss Villiers, he's married to that other tar-brushed gin, young Carwell — or he would be if he hadn't been able to get her without it."

How was more stung by that than by anything Boreman had said yet. "No bloody fear! I wouldn't use her for practice. Besides, she's your gin, isn't she?"

Boreman's opinion of Louise Carwell had better not be recorded. He turned back to Barbara. "I'll leave you with this beautiful thought, Miss Villiers. It may be a boy or it may be a girl — but, whatever it is, it'll be a bloody bastard!"

And, rolling his tongue with relish round the phrase, 'bloody bastard', Joe Boreman stalked out. It was the last thing he ever said.

How poured himself a drink; and then, as an afterthought, offered one to Barbara; she sipped at it, without looking at him, and when she put her glass down, he switched off the light.

Darkness covered her misery. She got up and moved to the door. He was somewhere in the background, silent.

"Aren't you going to say anything to me, Jack?"

"You'd better go home and get some sleep."

"What he said is true, I suppose?" She was pleading with him to deny Boreman's story.

"What does it matter at this time of night?"

"It matters all the time. I'm going to have a baby."

"So what?"

"What do you mean?"

"You won't be the first half-caste to have a bastard."

"I'm not a half-caste. I'm a quadroon."

"A distinction without a difference."

"That's a caddish thing to say to your wife."

"You're not my wife, though."

"If I'm not legally, I always was at heart. I loved you, Jack; and I thought you loved me. You've never been cruel like this to me before. Don't you love me, Jack?"

"I suppose I did," he conceded, moodily, "but this business has me gutzered. I've drunk too much tonight." Suddenly he flared up. "Damn those bloody natives. Why can't they shut up? They get on my nerves. I don't know what I'm saying half the time. Why did they choose this night of all nights to hold a *meke?*"

"It's not a *meke.* A *meke* is a ceremonial dance. They're singing carols."

"I don't care a damn what they call it in your bloody language. They're kicking up a bloody row, that's all I know. Why don't they shut up?"

She ignored that, asking helplessly, "What are we going to do, Jack?"

"Now you've told him, all the bloody burg will know."

"Yes, I'm sorry about that. But that makes it all the more important to decide what we're going to do."

"We can't talk about it now. You'd better go home. It's getting on for one."

She went towards him, and put her hands on his shoulders. He resisted slightly, and then allowed her to cling to him.

"You won't let me down, will you, Jack? I love you. I couldn't stand it if you stopped loving me."

Perhaps something in her tone frightened him, for he put his hands up and caressed her, and pleaded with her in his turn, "You won't split on me, will you, *loloma*? If I square Boreman to keep it dark, you won't tell anyone else, will you? That will put the pot on everything. You see that, don't you? I'll see you through all right. It's my child, I know it is. And we'll bring it up together. I oughtn't to have said the things I've been saying. I've been drinking too much, and you upset me by wanting to talk and putting me off my stroke. And when you told me about — the baby, I was so upset, I didn't know what I was saying. But I do love you, you know I do." He put his face to hers, and tried to kiss her, but she turned her mouth away.

178

"And you'll never say this is not your child?"

"Of course I won't, ducky. I'll never deny it."

"And you love me, don't you? Say you will always love me, Jack."

"I love you, loloma, and I will always love you."

She allowed him to kiss her then, but all the passion had gone. She wanted to believe him. She *must* believe him.

"Better?" he whispered. "Go home now, and we'll talk tomorrow, eh?" He kissed her, and then broke off to add, "If you don't let me down, I won't let you down, darling."

"You don't seem to realise that I love you, Jack. Now and for ever. You needn't be afraid that I'll let you down." She spoke with mingled bitterness and scorn, and as soon as he raised his mouth from hers, she twisted herself calmly out of his grasp and walked out without another word.

But she did not go far. She leaned against a tree some two hundred yards along the lane, wondering whether to kill herself or whether there was any alternative. If Jack no longer loved her — if he was concerned only for his own safety — she felt she did not want to live.

A quarter of a mile away, the Fijians were still singing carols. It was not the season for carols, but they enjoyed the tunes. Before the white men came, the *Kaivitis* chanted in unison, but they had no traditional songs in the European sense of the term; and now, when they gather round to sing, it is the hymns they have learned in the Mission schools that they love to render. Barbara felt herself attracted to this joyful music. She crossed a paddock until she came within throwing distance of her remote kinsfolk. They were squatting round in a large circle on a grassy expanse bordered by palms, lit here and there by kerosene lamps. Women and children mingled with the men in what was obviously a very informal sing-song.

Barbara sat down and drew her knees

up to her chin, so that her frock rucked up almost to her waist; and clasped her hands round her bare knees, resting her chin on her hands. A slender, long-legged girl of nineteen can sit thus without discomfort, although perhaps with some loss of dignity. The thought passed through her mind that it was years since she had sat thus, and she wondered if she was instinctively trying to guard the child in her womb.

One of the native women had a particularly clear and pure contralto voice and she took the lead now, while the women crooned softly, and the men growled a third lower.

"Once in Royal David's City
Stood a lowly cattle shed,
Where a Mother laid her Baby
In a manger for his bed."

Barbara was uplifted. Tears came into her eyes. To have a baby of her very own would indeed be sweet.

Fijians have good night eyesight, and a dignified old gentleman came over to her and gravely bade her 'Good evening'.

She scrambled to her feet and answered him in Fijian, returning his greeting and adding that she had been made so happy to hear the singing and wished to say 'Thank you' for it.

He complimented her on her command of his language; and she explained that she had spoken it from birth, that she too was a native of Viti Levu, that her great-grandfather had been a chief at Tailevu.

He insisted that she must join the circle, if only for a little while, and he led her to a place where she seated herself cross-legged *vaka viti* (Fiji fashion). A young man brought her the *yanggona bilo,* and she clapped her hands, intoning *'Bula! Bula!',* and then drank from it according to the rules, while the company clapped hands and shouted *'Vinaka! Vinaka!'*

They sang another carol, and when presently she rose to go, they all stood and sped her on her way with the Fijian song of farewell, *'Isa Lei'.* She joined in this song of love and parting, half weeping with the joy of their kindness and courtesy; and when, with the final verse, the young men suddenly beat fortissimo on the wooden *lalis*, she knew, as perhaps she had never known before, that Fiji was her homeland and the Fijians were her people.

As she walked up the hill towards Althorp, reflecting on the simple dignity of these natives and the crude cruelty of the white man she loved — she still loved him, and knew she would always love him — the contralto came smoothly across the tropic night —

"God be with you till we meet again!"

And presently the voice slid boldly into the tune known all over the English world as 'Eventide'. Barbara was too far away to hear the Fijian words, but she mentally fitted the English.

"Abide with me. Fast falls the eventide. The darkness deepens."

A clamour of gruff male voices then came thudding in with:

"Lord, with me abide!"

Sopranos chimed in with a throbbing

monotonous accompaniment. The soloist's clear bell arose above the booming of the men; her voice throbbed with emotion; she believed every word.

And the tune rose and fell, now in harmony, now in unison, now solo, now in full chorus. And the poor deluded girl stumbled on up the hill, her eyes blinded with tears of exaltation.

Sub-Inspector Capel reduced Barbara's narrative to a statement of facts, without quoting the actual words of dialogue or attempting to record her emotions; and she signed it with her right hand. Then she pointed to the cable from the Melbourne police.

"So you see, Mr. Spearpoint, when you showed me this, it wasn't news to me that he had a wife and children. I've known since Saturday night. But I didn't know that all his mother had was a small annuity, and that she would have left him nothing. He used to skite about some houses in Melbourne; but as I read this, they belonged to him, and he let his mother and wife share the rents."

"That's about the size of it."

"He told me a lot of lies." She said this without emotion, merely as a statement of fact.

Capel, still young enough to be influenced by the sight of beauty in distress, ventured to remark, "You can take that as a tribute to your virtue, can't you?" and was rewarded by a smile from her and a slight scowl from his superior officer.

Spearpoint asked, "What happened to the marriage certificate?"

"I have it here." She took a sealed envelope from her bag, and offered it to Spearpoint. He waved it away, but she insisted on his reading it. "Jack — Mr. How made me promise to keep it sealed up and never to show it to anyone, because if his mother heard — . Of course, I ought not to have told Mr. Boreman, but Jack had upset me, so — Well, it doesn't matter now. I'd rather you saw the certificate, Mr. Spearpoint. It proves my story."

Spearpoint slit open the envelope,

extracted a folded paper, read it and handed it back to her without comment. It certainly proved that she was justified in believing herself to be married.

"You were content to live in Malua indefinitely as a single woman?"

"I wasn't content — not at all. But — I know I was a fool — but I loved him and trusted him. The trouble was there was someone in Malua — I think now it was Boreman — who used to write to someone in Melbourne who knew his mother. We didn't know how she heard, but she certainly knew things that Jack didn't tell her. Jack was certain she couldn't last much longer. He was expecting to get a cable any day to say she'd gone. That was what he said, though I don't know what to believe now. He said that if we just hung out a little longer we'd be able to go and live in comfort in Australia. I suppose I'm not the first girl who's been taken in by — a man she loved."

"Nor the last." Spearpoint waited while she wiped her eyes and then asked her if she recognised the blue handkerchief.

"It's probably mine. I had one like that and I lost it on Saturday night. I certainly use this scent."

"Do you know anyone who had one just like it?"

"Mr. Anderton has one the same colour. But his wouldn't have scent on it, would it?"

Spearpoint thought: it might, if he'd wanted to pass it off as hers. He explained where the handkerchief was found.

"If I'd dropped it in Mr. How's room, someone could have picked it up and used it to hold the gun, couldn't they?"

"Of course. Whereabouts in the room would you have dropped it?"

"Somewhere between the bed and the door, I suppose. I sat on the chair on the left as you go in."

"Where was Mr. How's rug."

"The rug? I think that was on his trunk on the far side of the bed — that's where he kept it."

"You never went anywhere near the trunk?"

"No. I was on this side of the bed all the time."

"I see. Now, you mentioned Mr. Anderton just now. He has made a statement, which I think you ought to hear; and he ought to hear yours. Are you willing for him to come in, and for both statements to be read aloud to the two of you?"

She seemed puzzled. "I don't know what it's got to do with him."

"He says he saw you on Saturday night. Did you know he was at the bach while you were in Mr. How's room?"

This startled her. "I hadn't the faintest idea. If he's said anything that contradicts anything I said, I'd like to have it cleared up. And if you think it will help to find out who killed Jack, you can use my story in any way you please. But you'll make him promise not to gossip about me until I've decided what to do, won't you?"

When Anderton came in, Spearpoint said formally, "You two have given me statements which don't quite gee up. Do you agree, Mr. Anderton, that we should have both read out and compared — on the understanding that you both treat them as not to be repeated outside these four walls?"

Anderton turned towards the girl — and Spearpoint could not decide whether his look was one of love or of contempt — and answered, slowly, "I don't think anything Miss Villiers can say can disprove the truth of what I said." He turned back to Spearpoint. "You can read my statement to her if you like. It tells her things I haven't said to her — things she doesn't know about."

"My statement will tell you things you don't know, too."

Spearpoint warned them not to interrupt while the reading was going on, and Capel began with Anderton's story.

The young man sat with his hands deep in his trouser pockets and his eyes fixed on the floor; Barbara, after some show of surprise when her name was mentioned, stared, expressionless, out of the window. When Capel had finished, Spearpoint asked them if they had anything to say, but neither had.

Anderton became very restless during the reading of Barbara's statement, and kept looking towards her and then away; for most of the time she sat with her hands over her face, quite still, not weeping, but in an attitude of acute embarrassment.

At the end, Spearpoint asked her if she wished to amend the statement in any way.

She looked up at him and shook her head.

Anderton, asked in his turn, blurted out, "All I can say is, that if she was his wife, he was a cad to say about her the things he said about her to me."

"Yet," Spearpoint remarked, "no doubt you have both observed an important discrepancy. Whereas Miss Villiers says nothing about hearing the shot, and implies that she left the bach before it was fired, Mr. Anderton says positively that he saw her leave the bach after the shot."

"Yes," Anderton admitted wretchedly,

"that was what I thought. But I didn't see her actually come out of the bach. I saw her come along the side and go out into the lane. From what she says she came out of the bach a good time before."

"So you're not prepared to swear in Court that you saw Miss Villiers come out of the building after you heard the shot?"

"I'm prepared to swear that I saw a woman — well, someone dressed like a woman — come out of the compound and go into the lane towards Althorp. But it was a dark night. I couldn't see her clearly. I was some distance away. I took it for granted it was Miss Villiers, because I hadn't seen any other girl there." He clutched at a straw, turning to Barbara, who sat disdainfully silent as he attempted to qualify his accusation. "It might have been Joe Boreman's girl. She might have been in his room all the time. You didn't go into his room, did you?"

"Of course I didn't! How do I know who else were in and around the bach? I hadn't the slightest idea you were spying on me, for instance."

"I apologise for that," he pleaded, humbly. "If I'd known you were his wife — "

"Whether I was his wife or not, you had no call to go spying on me."

Spearpoint cut in, asking them in turn whether they had anything more to say. Neither had, so he dismissed them.

When they had gone, Capel remarked tentatively, "I was wondering if you were going to make an arrest, sir."

"Who should I arrest?"

"That's what I can't decide, sir. But could it be that they did it together, and agreed to tell slightly different stories?"

"I shouldn't think so. I'm not satisfied that either is telling the complete truth, but I can't see that we can hold them. Send Sergeant Tamata up to Mataiveithangge to see if he can get corroboration of the girl's story. Then we must scratch around for more facts. There are still some avenues unexplored."

"All the same, sir," sighed Capel,

reflectively, "I'd give quids to hear what they're saying to each other now."

Then the sergeant brought in a note for the Inspector, and the story of Saturday night at the bach was given a new twist.

10

The Story Sub-Inspector Capel Would Have Given Quids to Hear

ANDERTON followed Miss Villiers out of the Police Station and asked, with a protective air, "Where do you go now?"

"Home, of course." She looked at her watch. "Gosh! It's nearly five o'clock."

"Shall I ring for a taxi for you? — But, no! the police ought to provide a car after keeping you here all this time." He turned to go back.

"No, that's all right. I can walk. I'm used to walking."

She started in the direction of Althorp, but slowly enough not to give the appearance of leaving him standing.

"It's a long way, well over a mile, isn't it, and uphill?" he protested, falling into step. "Do you think you ought to walk all that way?"

"Why not? I often do."

"Well, I mean, you're not quite well, are you?"

"Walking won't do me any harm. Do me good. I'm in perfect health." She laughed a little ruefully.

"If you think so — . May I come with you?"

"If you like."

They followed the coast road for some way in silence. In her high-heeled shoes she was inches taller than he was, and she moved with an easy grace which he found both fascinating and disconcerting. He was a shy young man; to walk alongside this goddess and to be able to hold conversation with her tied his tongue in knots.

She broke the silence. "I've never been questioned by the police before. Inspector Spearpoint was very nice to me. I suppose he realised how upset I was."

"So he ought to be. All this must have been very distressing to you, especially after the way Jack How treated you."

She added, firmly, "And the way someone has treated him."

"Were you really in love with him?" He could not keep the jealous note out of his voice.

"Of course. I married him, didn't I?"

"He wasn't good enough for you."

"I couldn't agree with that."

"Of course he wasn't. Not within a thousand miles. Not that any man could ever be worthy of your love, but — "

She looked down at him with a smile. "That's nonsense, you know, Mr. Anderton."

"Why don't you call me Harry?"

"It's nonsense whatever I call you."

"I don't think so."

She changed the subject abruptly. "Who do you think can have — done it? I can't understand it at all. I can't see that anyone could have reason to kill them both."

"At first I thought they must have murdered each other, but Inspector

Spearpoint won't have that."

"Nor would I. I'd believe anything wicked of Boreman, but I'm sure Jack wasn't a murderer."

"How can you be sure?" he urged, roughly.

"It's just what I feel. After all, he was my husband. I knew him pretty well."

"But not enough!"

"That's different. Murder and bigamy aren't the same sort of thing. Only a wicked man would murder anyone; but a man might marry a girl because he — loved her more than his wife." Already in her mind she was idealising her relations with the dead man, and forgetting his crude cruelty at their final meeting. Then, he had been drunk and suffering from the shock of her disclosure.

There was a long break in the conversation, each pursuing thoughts in a different channel. Presently he asked, "What are you going to do now?"

"Now? — Oh, I haven't thought about that. Have the baby, I suppose, and then come back to the office, if they'll have me."

"I shouldn't think there'd be much doubt about that. All this is your misfortune, not your fault. What I meant was: you haven't thought of getting rid of it?"

Her tone showed that she was horrified. "Of course not! That would be — why, it would be murder, wouldn't it?"

He tried to justify himself and floundered more deeply. "I don't see why it shouldn't be done — when a woman's been — taken, against her will. That's not a crime."

"I should feel it was a crime to murder Jack's child. Besides, I wasn't taken against my will. Far from it. Jack was my husband. This child is all that's left to me of him."

"Yes, I see that," he conceded, hastily. "It's very noble of you. You're being generous to his memory." She did not respond to that, and he went on, "All the same, it's going to be very hard for you, having a child without a father."

"No harder than for any other widow."

"People won't think of you as a widow. You won't have a ring. You won't be entitled to his name."

"I haven't had time to think about that. I've got a certificate that I was married. I'm not sure that it would be right to produce it. All I'm sure of at the moment is that I'm going ahead with having Jack's child." She changed the subject with evident determination. "Will you go back to living at the bach?"

"I suppose I shall, when other fellows come to share it. I don't fancy living there alone."

"That's natural."

Silence fell again; he broke it with a desperate note in his voice which suggested that his speech was premeditated.

"You know, Barbara, my parents aren't wealthy. I can't pretend they are. My father's a teacher in an ordinary school in London. I don't expect to inherit anything; and I have nothing but what I earn."

"Most people are like that, aren't

they?" She was deliberately matter-of-fact. "Most of the people I know have nothing but debts and next month's salary to pay part of them with."

"Of course, I shall make more money when I've had more experience. I might try to qualify as an accountant. In a few years, I might not be doing so badly."

He hesitated in his nervousness long enough to give her the chance to steer the conversation into safer channels.

"Why did you come to Fiji, Mr. Anderton?"

"Harry!"

"Harry, then!"

"It was a bit unfortunate — except, of course, that if I hadn't come I'd never have met you."

"Not much good fortune in that."

"I think there is. The fact is, I lost my job in London when the firm I was working for was taken over by a rival, and I had an uncle in Auckland who had a business there — a one-man import-export business — and he offered me a job if I'd come out to New Zealand.

But he was killed in a motor accident just after I arrived, and the business collapsed. So I had to look for a job, and I was lucky enough to get taken on by Marryan & Cutt. Last year they sent me to Lautoka, but I didn't like it much, and I came to R. L. & Co. because I thought I'd like Malua better. That's all. I don't know whether I shall stay in the Islands. If things looked up at Home, I think I should go back. — You'd like to go to England, wouldn't you?"

"I'd like a trip, of course. Who wouldn't? But it would be rather cold after Fiji, wouldn't it? All right for you, brought up there. But I don't think I should ever want to leave the sun."

"You wouldn't be known there. You see, I'm thinking of you — and the baby. I feel so sorry for you."

"I feel sorry for myself, of course. Not that that's much good. This has happened to a lot of other girls, hasn't it? Perhaps I'm lucky, in a way, to have a baby. It's a piece of Jack that's still alive."

"You may think that now, when you don't realise what he's let you in for; there will be all sorts of problems and difficulties for a girl with a fatherless child."

She brushed them aside with, "I'll face them when they come."

A pause. Then he enquired tentatively. "You might marry someone else?"

She retorted tartly, "Who'd want to marry a girl with a fatherless child?"

He got it out then, shame-faced, a mere muttering.

"I would marry you — Barbara."

She did not answer that, but looked straight ahead, embarrassed, wishing he hadn't said it.

After waiting in vain for a sign that she had heard, he burst out in a torrent of words, "I'm sorry, Barbara, I didn't mean to give you the idea that I would marry you out of pity. That was all wrong. I want to marry you, Barbara, because I — because I love you. There! I've said it now. I love you, Barbara. I want to marry you for yourself. Not out of pity. I always have from the moment I first saw you, I would love and cherish you, and be faithful to you, too. Will you marry me, Barbara? Say you will. We could be married quite soon."

She halted, considering, and then rebuffed him, quietly, "It's an honour you do me, but — it wouldn't work."

"Why not?"

He tried to take her by the arms and turn her to face him, but she shook herself free.

"No — please!"

"But why not, Barbara? I love you, I tell you. I'd do anything for you." She shook her head slightly, embarrassed, not knowing what to say. He went on, almost aggrieved. "I know you don't like me much, and wouldn't come to the pictures when I asked you. But you had him then. If you knew me better, you'd come to like me. I'm sure you would, Barbara. You would; you know you would."

She looked down gravely at his anxious, flushed face, and answered with polite decision, "No, I'm sorry. I don't think so." She began to walk slowly on, not dismissing him, but rejecting his attempt to embrace her.

Again he asked, aggrieved, "Why not?"

"If you insist on an answer — . I'm sorry to have to say this: but I don't love you and I don't think I ever could."

"But I love you so much, Barbara, that I could make you love me in time."

"I don't think so. It's more likely that your feelings would change. You see, I don't believe you understand me at all. You don't really love me, you're attracted to my face and my body. You don't know the real me. If you ever came to know me properly, you wouldn't like me. We don't think alike at all. Your suggestion that I might want to have Jack's child — destroyed, that shocked me. It's a horrible thought. I couldn't marry a man who thought such a thing of me." She choked, and for a moment could not speak. "This baby — it's all I have to live for, now he's dead — don't you see?"

"I would love and cherish it as if it were my own. I promise you that, Barbara."

"I don't believe you could. You weren't a friend of Jack's. You didn't like him. Suppose this is a boy, and the dead ring of Jack. You couldn't love him — specially if he turns out to be dark. Do you realise that one of my grandmothers was a full-blooded Fijian? Suppose my child was a throwback to her, and yet obviously Jack's child, too: could you really love him as one of your own?"

"It's just as likely to be a girl, and as lovely as you are."

She said nothing to that, and he tried another argument.

"I see that your concern is with the child rather than with yourself. As things are, it will be born into an unkind world, and other children will mock it because it has no father. If you marry me — soon — the child would have a father and a name. No one need ever know who the real father was. Everyone would think it was me."

He brought this out as confidently as if he thought it was a master trump, instead of a king-sized revoke.

"You mean people would think I got married because I had to?"

"That happens all over the world, and people soon live it down. It's quickly forgotten."

"It may be like that at Home, but it isn't in Fiji. I've lived here nearly all my life, and I know."

"But would that be worse than things as they are? People won't believe you were married to Jack How."

"I know I was. That's the difference."

"I can't see much difference," he argued, moodily.

"Any girl can see the difference between being deceived into marriage by a bigamist, and marrying someone she doesn't love because she has to."

His tone was almost a snarl. "So it boils down to this, does it: that sooner than marry me, and take my name, you'd prefer to have your child known to everyone as a little bastard?"

She halted in her tracks, looked at him, and then walked on swiftly, saying over her shoulder, "You shouldn't have said that, Mr. Anderton, really you shouldn't. But it proves my point, doesn't it?"

"I don't see that," he caught up with her.

"Everything you say only goes further to prove that you don't understand me at all — that we could never get on happily together." She stopped and faced him. "I think, if I ever married again, and not for love, it would only be to a man I was sure would be kind to me."

"Meaning that I — "

She interrupted him with a gesture, and dismissed him with, "I'm nearly home now. I think we've both said enough. If we say any more, we shall only go on hurting each other. Don't think I'm ungrateful for your sympathy, and for the compliment of offering to marry me. But I'm sure we'd both be wretched. And thank you for coming all this way with me."

Her manner left him no room for

argument. He raised his topee and left her. He stumbled down the hill in an agony of insulted disappointment and frustrated desire. Barbara seated herself on a bench outside her house for half-an-hour and watched the western sky change from pale blue to violet and then to black; and not once did she think of Harry Anderton.

11

The Girl Tells a Different Story

"IT'S a queer thing, Capel," remarked Spearpoint, looking up from the note the sergeant had brought in, "but hardly any of our witnesses have come to us and volunteered information. Almost everyone has had to have the facts dragged out by forceps."

"And what we drag out aren't always the facts, sir. I think the reason we don't get voluntary witnesses is that everyone who knows what happened at the bach on Saturday night is afraid we'll find out the truth."

"Maybe; and the others don't realise they're in possession of facts we need. Anyway, here's two blokes who want to tell us something. Show 'em in, sergeant."

The two witnesses who now came into

the Inspector's office were contrasting figures well known along the West Coast. Jarvis Marplesdon, six foot four, and Dirck Stoop, five foot two, were partners in a nondescript business, turning their hands to everything legitimate from boat-building to supplying parrots to tourists. They were as mixed in blood as men born in the South Sea Islands could be, and famed as comic, honest and hard-working citizens.

They entered shame-faced, ill-at-ease, each trying to hide behind the other and egg him forward. Once in, they perched nervously on the very edges of the chairs Capel offered, and then glanced at each other, doubtful who should explain their presence. A less experienced officer than Inspector Spearpoint might well have assumed that he was about to receive a complete confession to the crimes.

"You have something to tell us about the deaths of Jack How and Joe Boreman?" he prompted, looking at Dirck.

Jarvis promptly nodded to Dirck, and Dirck nodded to the Inspector. Dirck then waved his hand towards the window and managed to articulate two words.

"Pigeon shooting."

The large single-paned window looked out on to the mill; behind the mill was a narrow belt of sugar-cane, beyond the canefield sprawled rugged hills, and beyond rose the mountains and forests of the interior — the haunt of the succulent, over-sized pigeons which were a delicacy down on the coast.

"You mean the two of you have been pigeon-shooting up in the hills, eh?"

Dirck nodded again, adding, "Heard about it when we came home."

"You went along the lane behind the bach on Saturday night, eh?"

Dirck nodded and smiled; Jarvis shook his head.

This puzzled Spearpoint for a moment; then inspiration came and he asked a third leading question. "Oh! I see. Dirck went along the lane, but Jarvis didn't, eh?"

Dirck opened his mouth to say, "Yup", thought caution preferable, and nodded.

Jarvis ventured to commit himself to speech, explaining, "My boy in hospital. Took him pineapples."

"I hope he's going on all right?"

In his gratitude, Jarvis made his longest speech of the day, "Thank you, sir, yes. He is well. He will be better soon."

"Glad to hear it. What did you see in the lane, Dirck?" Dirck, more at ease, explained that he had gone along the lane to recover a gun he had lent to a man who lived at Althorp.

"What time did you pass the bach?"

Dirck held out his wrist to indicate that he had no watch.

"Did you hear any noise at the bach?"

"'Frankie and Johnny' at the bach. 'Good King Wenceslas' on the beach."

"Then you didn't hear a revolver shot at the bach?"

"No revolver shot. Saw girl crawling under the bach."

"You saw a girl crawl *under* the bach?"

Dirck nodded and smiled. He had played his trump.

Spearpoint dragged the story out sentence by sentence. As he passed the bach, Dirck, with his keen night eyes, saw a girl creeping surreptitiously along the lane towards him. As he came nearer, she halted and stood quite still, so he walked past pretending he had not seen her in the darkness. But he was curious to know why she was trying to hide from him. So presently, he turned and tracked her as if she had been a pigeon. From a distance he saw the girl climb through the fence into R. L. & Co.'s compound, and from nearer he saw her crawl under the bach at Joe Boreman's end.

Jarvis, closely questioned, insisted that Dirck had told him this strange story immediately after they had met on Saturday night, and that they had wondered greatly at it. As soon as they had returned home and heard of the murders, they had decided that the Inspector must be told.

Finally, Spearpoint asked the 64,000 dollar question.

"Did you see who the girl was?"

To his surprise, Dirck named the wrong girl.

"Louise Carwell, it was."

"Are you sure?"

"Known her since she was a filly."

"Now, Louise, when you came here last evening you did not tell us the entire truth."

"I did so!"

"I want the truth this time."

"You had it last time."

"Louise: you were seen in the compound, close to the bach, shortly before the shot was fired."

"What if I was?"

"Then the story you told me yesterday was not true. Are you going to tell us the truth now, or do you prefer to be arrested and to stand your trial for murder?"

"I didn't murder either of them!"

"But you know who did?"

"Of course I do. I'll tell you."

"The truth this time, if you please."

The second story told by Miss Carwell, like the second story told by Miss

Villiers, was sometimes incoherent; her emotions, too, were implied rather than expressed in the words she used. But this was the story she was trying to tell.

Louise was frantically and with good reason jealous of Barbara Villiers, so when she saw Barbara walking towards the bach she decided to follow. Convinced that Barbara would be in Jack How's room, she climbed through the fence at Boreman's end of the building and crawled underneath until she calculated she was directly under How's room. Here, she overheard part of the dialogue between the lovers and most of the conversation which followed Boreman's invasion. It filled her with hatred and with gloating satisfaction.

She could not hear all the final exchanges between the girl and How, because the girl spoke very softly, and How sometimes dropped his voice; but she gained a savage triumph from hearing her rival sobbing.

Barbara went, and Louise heard How's

footsteps above. She was wondering what to do next when she realised that there had been complete silence above her for several minutes. This silence was suddenly shattered by the report of the revolver at the other end of the building.

As she lay there in fear and dismay, she became conscious that the native drums on the beach were being thudded with renewed vigour. It was almost like a triumphal march after ritual murder.

The drums died down presently, and Louise ventured out of her hiding-place. It was perhaps a quarter of an hour after the shot that she stood upright at the foot of the stairs leading up to How's room. She was surprised to see torchlight in there.

She must have made some noise, for the torch was shut off, and How came to the doorway, calling out, "Who's there?"

Louise answered, her voice shaking, "It's me, Mr. How. What's happened?"

He came forward, directing the torch at her, asking, "Who are you?" She could see his white body gleaming in the dark; he had nothing on but pyjama trousers and canvas shoes.

"Louise — Louise Carwell, Mr. How."

He switched off the torch, asking roughly, "What are you doing here?"

"I was in the lane and I heard a noise. What's happened?"

"That fool Boreman's rigged up a booby-trap and shot himself. That's all. Nothing to worry about, girl."

She ventured on to the veranda, close to him.

"You're all right yourself, Mr. How?"

"Of course I'm all right. I was in my room. He shot himself. Didn't I tell you?"

"What did he shoot himself for?"

"How the hell should I know?" How chuckled. "Maybe he suddenly realised that nobody loved him."

Louise was inflamed with jealousy and hatred and desire. She did not believe a word of what he said. She thought that he must have killed Boreman because Boreman knew that he was a bigamist —

and that he would kill her too if she revealed that she also knew the guilty secret. It was delicious to be in such danger, and yet to be confident of being clever enough to survive.

"Let me see," she demanded.

"It's a horrid sight. Bullet went right through his ruddy head. Blood all over the place."

"What are you going to do about it?"

"You can leave that to me, girl. You'd better clear off before anyone knows you're here."

Louise asked again to be shown the body and the booby-trap, and when How refused she argued, "How can I know you didn't shoot him yourself?" She made to push past.

"Don't be a little fool!" He grabbed her by the shoulders and pulled her into his room.

This was more deliciously dangerous than ever. She was close to the murderer now, closer than she had ever been to him, almost as close as she had ever dreamed of being. But his breath smelt of beer and he was half twisting her arm and hurting her; and she was hating him for spurning her devoted love and seducing the big-bosomed Villiers bitch.

She struggled to wrench herself free. "How do I know you didn't kill him yourself?" she repeated.

"Listen, love, be reasonable; you know I wouldn't do such a thing." He swung her round into his arms and closed her mouth in a long kiss. She squirmed and wrestled, but it was useless to resist. She felt herself melting in his grasp. The native drums were thudding on the beach. Her pulses were throbbing with animal desire. She lay eager and passive in his arms.

He released her so unexpectedly that she almost fell.

"I want to see," she said sullenly.

He caught her two hands, held her off, and whispered, "His head is all bloody, love. You wouldn't want to see that. You'd dream about it for weeks. You run along home and leave everything to your Uncle Jack."

She was furiously angry in her disappointment. She tried to wrench her hands free, and beat at him with her fists.

"What's the matter, you little tiger?"

"You beast! You murderer! You've murdered Boreman and now you're trying to murder me!" Her voice rose almost to a scream and he released a wrist in order to clap a hand over her mouth.

She bit him.

They wrestled fiercely in the dark, and he twisted her round, and bent her over the bed with her face buried in the pillow, so that she feared he would suffocate her. But he squeezed a hand firmly across her mouth, and the other imprisoned her wrists behind her; and leaning over her, he argued with her in the darkness of the throbbing night.

"Stop screaming, girl! You don't want to bring the whole town round us, do you? If you want to see a bloody corpse, I'll show you one. But you must stop screaming."

He jerked her to her feet, removing

his hand from her mouth, asking, "O.K. now?"

She gulped in breath, and then whispered sulkily, "Let go my hands, then."

He shifted his grip, so that she was in front of him, with his hands on her shoulders, and thus he marched her along the veranda.

(He had marched his other quadroon visitor in the same way an hour earlier, but Louise did not know this.)

"It's a horrid sight!" he whispered into her ear, gloating. "He looks even more horrible than he did alive. Blood! You're sure you want to see it?"

With each step, she became more terrified. She struggled to free herself, but he held her firmly. Why she did not scream for help, she did not know; perhaps because this was a personal battle. She hated him and feared him, and yet he kept her fascinated and angry with desire.

At Boreman's doorway he whispered, "I won't shine the torch on to his head. I'll show you the gun on the floor.

There's a string tied to the trigger. You can see it going under the pillow. The gun was wedged in a drawer, wrapped in that blue handkerchief you see hanging there. See! When he put his head on the pillow it jerked a cord tied to the bed-post on the far side and that pulled the trigger; he was shot right through the head and died at once. A perfectly planned and executed suicide. Understand?"

"Yes," she gasped. She was leaning back with her head in the hollow of his naked shoulder. He switched the torch on and ran the light round the chest of drawers and the floor, showing all he had described, and the blood dripping from the bed and forming a pool under it.

She put her hand over her mouth to stifle a scream.

"Enough, love?"

"I — I don't know."

He ran the beam along the floor to the foot of the bed and then raised it slowly so that she saw a foot sticking up under the sheet, then the raised knee of the other leg, then the dishevelled sheet around the waist, and the shirt with one pocket bulging full. The light stopped at the pocket. Drums in the night thudded on her nerves.

"No!" She turned and hid her face on his shoulder. She had seen more than she could bear.

"You don't want to see his ghastly death grin?"

"No, no, no!"

He switched the light off and pulled her roughly away. She came unresisting, hardly able to walk for the horror of what she had *not* seen.

Now she was half swooning in his arms, and he kissed her again, and again desire for him overcame all her hatred and her horror, so that she strained to lead him into his room, a victim willing for the taking.

But he released her at the top of the steps, whispering, as if to a refractory child, "So now you'll go home and forget all about this and leave everything to your Uncle Jack, eh?"

223

She began to cry with rage, disappointment and hurt pride.

"Come, come, little girls should be asleep in bed."

He gave her a friendly slap and impelled her down the steps.

She went without protest; but she did not go far. She started to walk straight forward towards the sea, but after the darkness had swallowed her, she faltered. Uncontrollable weariness overcame her. She could hardly move her feet. She sank down on the ground, and punched the earth in an abandonment of rage and despair.

The natives on the beach were singing *Isa Lei* — a full harmonious choir of sixty voices, the women's shrill and high, and the men growling deep in their chests. The tune was the theme song of the land of her birth, but it did not soothe or exalt her. It filled her with bitterness to compare her misery with the singers' happiness.

All strength had gone from her limbs, and she lay there full-length, wallowing in her wretchedness.

In the bach, everything was dark and silent. She wondered what Mr. How was doing, but too idly to care.

She became aware of a figure gliding along the side of the building — a tall woman. The night was too dark and Louise was too far away to distinguish details, but she had no doubt that it was the girl Villiers.

The woman tiptoed up the veranda steps, and glided out of sight. Presently she reappeared, glided down the steps and out into the lane. How long she had been there, Louise could not tell. Long enough for whatever foul deed she had committed.

Louise lay there a long time, her mood changing from rage to immeasurable grief. The native singing ceased, and all Malua was covered by the darkness of the tropic night. Only the throbbing of the electric light plant showed that somewhere man was awake and active.

At last, she scrambled to her feet, intending to go home, She skirted round the bach with a shudder; and when she had gone a couple of hundred yards along the lane, and was almost at her own gate, she heard a scream from the bach.

It unnerved her completely. She ran straight to her room, and collapsed in a paroxysm of sobbing.

When Louise had signed the statement Capel drafted from her narrative, Spearpoint asked her impressively, "That is the complete truth, is it?"

She protested defiantly. "Yes, I told you it was!"

"You said at the start that you knew who killed Mr. Boreman. You don't really know, do you?"

"Mr. How killed him!"

"Why are you so sure Mr. Boreman didn't kill himself in the way Mr. How described to you?"

"Because I heard the girl Villiers telling Mr. How she was in the family way, and then she told Mr. Boreman they were married, and Mr. Boreman said that in that case Mr. How could

226

go to prison for bigamy; and after Mr. Boreman had gone back to his room, Mr. How and the girl Villiers were whispering together, and Mr. How said something about her helping him to keep Mr. Boreman's mouth shut. She must have helped him to work out the booby-trap and then she went away while Mr. How shot Mr. Boreman and then she came back and smothered Mr. How."

"One thing at a time. You still haven't explained why it was impossible for Mr. Boreman to have committed suicide."

"It was the girl Villiers' handkerchief that was used to hold the gun to prevent fingermarks showing; if Mr. Boreman had shot himself he wouldn't have wanted to hide the fingermarks, would he?"

"How do you know it was Miss Villiers' handkerchief?"

"Because I've seen it often, that's how. She must have lent it to Mr. How for the purpose."

Spearpoint stared at her sceptically.

She jumped to her feet and pounded the desk with her fist, screaming, "And the girl Villiers came back after that and murdered Mr. How!"

"Forgetting her handkerchief?"

Louise calmed down, saying knowingly, "The criminal always forgets something, doesn't she?"

"Indeed she does," Spearpoint concurred. He considered for a moment. "You were friendly with Mr. How yourself once, weren't you?"

"Sort of" she admitted.

"Did he ever ask you to marry him?"

"You've no right to ask that!"

"You mean: he didn't?"

She coloured but did not answer.

"You never had reason to believe he might marry you?"

That goaded her to anger again. "He would have if the girl Villiers hadn't made herself cheap to him!"

"I see. But he seduced you?"

"How dare you say that!"

"You mean: he did?"

"No, he did not!"

"And everything happened on Saturday night exactly as you said?"

228

"Yes, it did!"

"Can you prove he never seduced you?"

She glared at him, and then sank back and put her hands over her face and whispered, "Yes, I can."

There was a long silence. Then Louise started up and turned to Capel. "He put the girl Villiers in the family way, and she smothered him with his rug!" She collapsed in a fit of weeping.

Spearpoint stood up. "Miss Carwell," he said formally, "a great deal of what you have told me has been corroborated from other sources. But not all of it. Are you sure that you have told me the complete truth, and kept nothing back this time?"

"Of course I have! Are you calling me a liar?"

"All I am prepared to say at the moment is that if on reflection, you remember something else you have not told me, or wish to correct anything you have said, I shall be happy to listen."

"There's nothing else to say!" She flounced out in a fury of insulted indignation.

Capel asked tentatively. "Could she have killed them both, sir?"

"It's certain she saw Boreman's body. No one she can have spoken to knows he went to bed with the money in his pocket, or that he was found with one knee sticking up. But she hasn't told us the whole truth yet."

"Her imagination ran away with her, don't you think, sir? I'm sure she was putting it on a bit when she said the sight of the blood nearly made her faint with horror. You remember that dog that was run over down by the wharf a few weeks back? That was enough to make a nice girl sick. Guts hanging out, and so on. But Miss Louisa was in the front of the crowd, and she wasn't turning a hair."

"She must have seen too many sights of that kind to be squeamish. And there are at least four other reasons why I believe some of her story is lies."

"I can think of two of 'em, sir; what are the others?"

Spearpoint told him.

12

The Accountant's Story

THE combing of Malua for traces of Joe Boreman's wife had been proceeding all day, and the sergeant in charge now presented his report. The number of households in or near Malua which might conceivably have given hospitality to a woman of her type was small, and enquiry had removed suspicion from all but one — and that a house which was temporarily closed. This was not surprising, for it was owned by Harry Bulkeley, a part-European who scratched up most of his livelihood by chartering out a small sea-going craft he owned and skippered; his wife often sailed with him, and they were sometimes away for weeks at a time. But what was unusual was that both his car and his ship were missing; he rarely used both at once.

One possible line of investigation there was temporarily out of order. Katerina, the Fijian girl who helped Mrs. Bulkeley with the housework and lived on the premises, was somewhere at sea with a family fishing party; they had set out on Sunday morning, and no one knew whether Katerina had been at the Bulkeleys' house on Saturday night or not.

The patient listing of everyone who might have been in the lane behind the bach at the time the unknown woman had enquired for Boreman had produced a number of vague statements.

A native constable on patrol along a road near Bulkeley's house had seen a big woman in European dress walking towards the bach at 11.40 hours. The night was dark and he did not look at her with any care, for he had taken her for Mrs. Fell, the doctor's wife, who was a big woman and a conscientious pedestrian; he had been mildly hurt at her not greeting him as she passed.

Spearpoint picked up the telephone and asked for a number.

An alluring voice answered, "I'm sorry: Dr. Fell's out on a call. Can I take a message?"

"It's George here. It was you I wanted."

"You shouldn't ring me when the doctor's out, George. Anyway, I have a complete alibi for Saturday night."

"That was what I suspected. Look! I'm trying to trace a strange woman, and I was wondering if — "

"My husband tells me I'm a strange woman, but you wouldn't know about that, George."

"You're not strange the way I mean. The woman I'm looking for is five foot nine inches tall, and her vital measurements have been given to me as 50–48–60."

"That can't be me. I'm at least four inches less than that — everywhere. And three inches taller."

"Quite."

"What do you mean: quite?"

"I mean that someone saw this other

woman and thought she was you."

"Tell me who it was and I'll come and sit on his lap and squash him." Mrs. Fell laughed. "Seriously, George, I wasn't out on Saturday night." She went on to name the highly respectable members of the community who had been visiting her house to play bridge and had stayed until half past twelve.

Spearpoint thought it hardly worth while to check her statement; for the next witness was a small Indian boy whose family occupied a shack (built of flattened petrol tins nailed to wooden supports) adjacent to the Indian *dhobi's* place, and who had wandered out to listen to the distant natives on the beach. He had seen a large *memsahib* walking away from the direction of the bach. He had wondered to see a *memsahib* walking: he thought *memsahibs* always moved about in cars. She had passed close to a lamp standard and he had noticed that one side of her face was dark brown though the other side was pink. He had no idea what the time was.

A variety of witnesses, of varying social backgrounds and degrees of reliability and vagueness, remembered seeing a big woman in European dress on Saturday evening either near the mill or over on the Bulkeleys' side of town. More definite was the evidence of the chief accountant at the mill, whose story was one the sergeant thought Spearpoint should hear personally.

The accountant was a man to be trusted, a New Zealander of forty-odd.

"Your three-striper tells me you're enquiring about a ten-ton Samoan woman with a ruddy great burn on one side of her mug."

"That's right."

"I can give you the good oil on her all right. She was toddling along the lane at the back of the mill about half after six on Sunday morning."

"Sunday morning?"

"Yesterday. I was driving to mass and saw her full on as she stepped aside and waited for me to pass. It was just on that bend where the road narrows."

"Which way was she going?"

"Away from the bach. Of course, I didn't know then what had happened at the bach, but anyway this was full daylight, long after those two poor cows had been done in. But if you're interested in her, I remember something that struck me as funny. As I came towards her, she turned her face away, and sort of gestured to hide her handbag behind her. After I'd passed, I looked back at her in the mirror, and she was staring after me, and I could see the burn mark on her face. Of course, it wasn't the ruddy burn that made me look twice at her. It was her size. She was a whopper."

"How was she dressed?"

"Fancy asking a mere man that! That's where you've got me. European, of course. I seem to remember a shady hat. Light dress, I think. Didn't really notice a thing but her weight and that ruddy great burn."

One further scrap of evidence had been extracted with difficulty from an itinerant peanut seller, who had a bad police record and who had previously been caught out in telling the police what he thought they wanted to hear rather than the truth. He alleged that he had passed the Bulkeleys' house about eight on Saturday evening, and had seen lights in the building and a car in the open-fronted shed.

Spearpoint consulted his opposite number in Suva, who said at once, "I haven't picked up a trace of Mrs. Boreman, Spearo, but I can give you the good oil on Harry Bulkeley. He cleared for Tonga with a mixed cargo about an hour before the *Duchess of Cleveland* docked; and his missus and Mrs. Curson were on the wharf waving 'em off. I don't need to tell you Mrs. Curson is the mate's wife and some sort of cousin of Mrs. Bulkeley, do I?"

"You don't. Are they still in Suva? Can you find out if Bulkeley's car was parked nearby, and if Mrs. Boreman went off in it?"

"I'll get the bloodhounds on to that, Spearo." He came back a couple of hours later to report that the car had been parked opposite the Customs' shed, but that he had been unable to find anyone who had seen it driven away. Enquiries at the hotels and of the part-European community had not produced any evidence of where Mrs. Bulkeley and Mrs. Curson were.

Spearpoint's next call was to the District Inspector whose territory included the coast settlement of Boscobal, where the Cursons lived; and presently his colleague's welcome voice confirmed his guess.

"You were right, Spearo. Mrs. Boreman and Mrs. Bulkeley are here with Mrs. Curson. They're all cousins of sorts. They all tell the same story: they met Eliza on the wharf, and got into Bulkeley's car and drove round here and have been indoors ever since. Mrs. Boreman said she caught a touch of influenza on the trip, and hasn't felt like going about. She says she intended going on to Malua to see her husband when Bulkeley gets back, but now he's dead, she doesn't know what to do. She seems quite cut-up about him, though she admits she hasn't seen him for years."

"Any independent corroboration?"

"No. There isn't another house near, and it's rather shut in, anyway. I'll make some enquiries, if you like."

"She was in Malua on Saturday night; and Bulkeley's car is said to have been in his shed then. You might ask if anyone saw it on the Malua road on Saturday afternoon or Sunday morning."

"Can do. Will you come and question her yourself?"

"Can't spare the time. But if you can get proof she did come this way, take out a search warrant and see what you can find."

"What ought I to find?"

Spearpoint told him.

Capel, who had been beckoned out of the office by the duty sergeant, came back with the news that Harry Bennet had escaped from the hospital.

The tall, bearded Punjabi constable set to guard Bennet had obeyed his instructions to the letter (as all constables who served

Spearpoint quickly learned to do). As soon as everyone was tucked up for the night, he had shouted to the night sister that he was going away for a meal and would be back in exactly one hour. He then looked in on the patient-prisoner as if to satisfy himself that he was in bed, and clumped off down the corridor as noisily as his steel-shod police boots would permit.

Emerging into the open, he tiptoed, with exaggerated caution, round the side of the building, and hid himself as completely as his girth allowed behind a palm tree some few yards from the window of Harry Bennet's room.

Contrary to normal hospital practice but in conformity with Spearpoint's request, the dirty clothes Bennet had been wearing when he was brought in had been left on a hook in his room. Harry fell into the trap thus baited, and soon the constable saw him clambering out of the window and making off into the night.

The constable followed as circumspectly

as he could; but his quarry moved with unexpected speed. It was only because Bennet was unsuspicious and did not look behind him at all that he did not detect that he was being followed. Having spent most of the day comfortably sleeping, he was as fit as he was ever likely to be.

It had been easy to bring to the Police Station the news that Spearpoint's ruse had succeeded, and that Harry was leading the constable a brisk walk along the Malua lanes; whether it would be easy or difficult to make contact with that constable would depend on whether the trail led to any of the places Bennet was expected to make for.

Leaving Capel at the office to serve as a communication centre, Spearpoint drove along the shore road to R. L. & Co.'s compound, parked his car in the shadow of the store, and followed the path to the bach as unostentatiously as his desire for speed would allow.

Pausing behind a tree within sight of the black bulk of the bach, he surveyed it carefully. No telltale torchlight indicated a visitor in the deserted building.

He looked round for the hidden constable guarding that side, and was gratified when a voice whispered from the dark, *"Nigh, sahib."* It was the agreed word indicating that no one had entered the bach from the front.

Spearpoint sidled past the building and into the lane. As he tiptoed along everything was so still that he again wondered if his sentry was on the job. At the point where the constable should have been, he halted, and raised his hand.

"Sahib!" came the thick whisper from the hedge.

"Ha?" ("Yes?")

The constable explained briefly that Bennet and his pursuer had not entered the lane. They had gone up the hill towards Althorp.

Spearpoint made a gesture of acknowledgment, and went on, past the Carwells' home, and up the hill. There was less need for concealment now. If Harry

Bennet discovered that he was being followed to his house, little harm could result. It was only if he had stolen the money from Boreman's pocket and was trying to remove it from its temporary cache that it was necessary to track him in secrecy until the pounce. The constable, however, had not been told this; and he had reasonably halted at the bend in the road that was so brightly lit by a lamp standard that he could not have ventured there without being seen for certain if Bennet so much as glanced over his shoulder.

Within view of the corner was an irregular row of bungalows, all occupied by part-Europeans. The ground was bumpy and scrubby, unfit for sugar-cane or any other bulk cultivation, and so had been leased in sections to citizens who were outside the full pale of European society without being condemned to either the native village or the Indian settlement.

Leaving the constable in the shadows, Spearpoint worked his way round to the back of Bennet's house, in the hope of satisfying himself that he was there. The ground was uneven; he dared not use his torch, and he had to step with caution, but he got into the paddock behind the houses without mishap.

There were no lights in the first house, which was the Villiers'. Barbara was perhaps on one of her long night walks. Her mother might well be next door. There was light enough, and steel guitars throbbing across the darkness.

In the third house were lights, but no noise. This was the Bennets'. But lights blazing from neighbouring houses prevented Spearpoint from getting close enough to see in. He had to be content to take station where he could be certain of seeing Bennet if he came out and started back to the hospital.

The Villiers' house was secluded. By day the garden was bright with flamboyant trees; and a hibiscus hedge shut off the neighbours. Some traveller palms and banana clumps cut the lamplight into strange distorted shapes.

Spearpoint was not looking that way;

but suddenly a woman screamed from the garden.

He heard bodies and feet scuffling on the concrete; and he ran forward in time to see a woman collapsing on the ground and the figure of a man thrusting his way furiously through the palms towards the road.

He shouted to Singh to "Stop that man!", and charged towards the fallen woman.

It was minutes before he could reach her across the uneven ground and the wire back fence; and two youngsters from next door were before him.

Barbara Villiers lay face downwards on the concrete path, with the haft of a knife sticking up between her shoulders.

13

Mrs. Boreman's Story

AS he ran towards the woman on the path, Spearpoint pulled his handkerchief from his pocket, and his first action on reaching her, recognising who she was and that she was still alive, was to grasp the upper part of the knife blade with the handkerchief and to tug it gently out. It came so easily that he was satisfied that the knife could not have penetrated any vital part. It had indeed not gone at all deep; but there was enough blood to satisfy the swiftly gathering crowd.

Mrs. Villiers displayed surprising fortitude and common sense. Without wasting time on emotional display, she knelt down and tore her daughter's dress open at the back. It then appeared that the point of the knife had struck a concealed button and had been deflected, so that it had slid sideways into the outer flesh. But, in falling, the girl had hit her forehead on the concrete. She was bleeding from the nose and from a mysterious cut on the cheek. Her right knee was damaged. She was unconscious and evidently a hospital case.

Spearpoint knew that no one in Althorp had a telephone, so he called for volunteers to dash down to the town on a bicycle and call the ambulance. Three young lads set out for the hospital at once, making a race of it, and nearly becoming ambulance cases themselves on the way.

Meanwhile, someone fetched a rug and Mrs. Villiers had her daughter moved on to it, and then she tied a pad over the wound in her back. There seemed to be no immediate danger, but the concussion might mask something not obvious.

Constable Singh came forward crestfallen. He had heard the scream and his officer's command to chase the assailant. But he had been badly placed for such a manoeuvre, and he had caught no more than a glimpse of the fugitive, who had swerved off the road on to a path leading across country to the east. Singh had started in pursuit, but had given up the chase as hopeless once he lost sight of the quarry and realised that he had choice of half-a-dozen tracks. He had been unable to judge the size of the man, but his impression was of someone not very tall, with a black head, khaki trousers and shirt and dark shoes.

"He ran fast, Inspector Sahib. He went for his ruddy life!"

Spearpoint and Mrs. Villiers rode in the ambulance with Barbara, who recovered consciousness as they went over a bad jolt. Her mother bent over her and cautioned her, "Don't try to talk, Babs. You'll be all right."

"Someone sprang at me," she murmured. "My head aches."

She shut her eyes, and it seemed that she lost consciousness again; but Spearpoint could not be certain of that. She had observed him, and she might not be willing to let him question her until she had had time to compose her answers.

He hung about in the corridor while the hospital took charge of her. Presently, Dr. Fell came out to him.

"Sorry, Spearo, but she's got concussion, and she mustn't be excited at present. She'll recover all right, and you can have a talk with her tomorrow."

Spearpoint did not waste time in arguing over what he had thought all along was inevitable; but he asked, "Did you notice that she is pregnant?"

"Not obvious. Are you sure? How long?"

"Three months, she said. I'll tell you a secret, but keep it under your hat. She was married to Jack How six months ago. She'll be worrying about the baby. You ought to be prepared to reassure her."

"There's no obvious reason why it shouldn't be all right. But thanks for the tip."

Spearpoint turned away. The night sister beckoned.

"Harry Bennet's back. I'm not sure

what time he climbed in the window, but he was all happy in bed by ten."

"He mustn't on any account get out again tonight."

"He won't, Mr. Spearpoint. Shall I give him something to keep him asleep until morning?"

"I'd like to talk to him first. But I must have Capel with me. I'll wait a bit."

The sister, who was not quite so good-looking as Barbara, but was pretty enough to satisfy most men, asked pertly, "You need a bodyguard? Afraid he'll knife you too?"

"You mustn't think he's ever knifed anybody. No. What he has to say for himself has to be taken down in case it has to be used in evidence, and two of us have to be present."

"I see. I can say what I like to one policeman, but if I ever have two together, I'd have to be careful?"

"In your case, sister, you should be more careful with one than with two."

"You said that, Inspector, I didn't."

When the two police officers came into

his room and turned on the light, Harry Bennet pretended to be asleep; and when he admitted to being awake he pretended to be surprised at recognizing who his visitors were.

"What do you want with me at this time of night?" he asked, with a not very convincing show of confidence.

"We want a full account of how you spent the last two hours, and I warn you that anything you say will be taken down and may be used in evidence."

He attempted to make an ill-timed and possibly obscene joke, but Spearpoint cut him short.

"Look, Bennet: we know you got out of bed, put on your togs, climbed out of the window and went up to Althorp. What did you do there?"

Bennet was unabashed. "I wondered if you'd have me trailed. I never looked round, did I?"

"You did not."

"I thought that if I looked round and saw a bobby, he'd have to nab me, but so long as I didn't know he was there,

251

he might let me go ahead."

"What did you go to Althorp for?"

"To speak to my wife, of course."

"Which way did you come back?"

"Don't you know? — Well, across the paddock behind my house, along the track beside the canefield, and over the hill."

"Why didn't you come back the way you went?"

"There was a hell of a rumpus in the road — a woman screaming and I don't know what the hell! If I'd gone out the front, I'd have been seen for certain, so when the row started I said to my missus, 'Here's my chance to nip out the back way without anyone seeing me'; and that's the way I went."

"You've no idea who it was who screamed, or why?"

"No flaming business of mine."

"A man went up to Althorp tonight, Bennet, hid in the Villiers' garden, and, when Barbara came home, he jumped on her, slashed her face with a knife, stabbed her in the back, flung her down on to the path and then made off into the bush!"

"My god! The devil!" The expressions of astonishment and anger which followed each other across Bennet's face were ample evidence that he was not that man. "Poor Barbara! Is she all right?"

"She'll be all right. The wound wasn't deep. What do you know about the attack?"

The insinuation roused him to indignant anger. "Do you think I'd try to stab a girl? And why should I? Who'd want to stab Barbara anyway? She's a decent kid. Of course it wasn't me. I was with my missus."

"She is in some way connected with the business at the bach on Saturday night. At least, she was in the lane. She may have seen the murderer. She may be a vital witness — or be thought to be one."

"Then it's no flaming business of mine, Inspector. I'm damned sorry about her. I'm glad she'll be all right. But you can't pin this on to me, either."

"Did you see anyone lurking in the bushes by the entrance to the Villiers' house?"

"No. I didn't look. I think the house was all dark. There was a party next door, as per usual."

"Did anyone see you go into your house, or come out? Is there anyone beside your wife who can swear you were in your house when Barbara screamed?"

Bennet thought. "I don't know that there is. I didn't see any of the neighbours, so I don't know if any of them saw me. The kids were all asleep at home. My missus can tell you I was with her for ten or fifteen minutes. There were plenty of lights about; someone may have seen me either coming or going."

"Did you see anyone on your way back to the hospital?"

"I don't think so."

"All right. Now, why did you go up to Althorp?"

"I've told you: to see my wife."

"You saw her this morning, and you'll be seeing her tomorrow. What was the importance of seeing her tonight?"

"I had something special to say to her. This morning I had a perishing copper listening to every flaming word I said. If you take me to clink tomorrow you'll listen to everything I say to her then. What I had to say was private and not for flaming coppers to listen to."

"Such as where to find the *Frances Teresa* money?"

Bennet seemed genuinely astonished. "Of course not. I don't know where the ruddy money is any more than you do! What I had to tell the missus was no ruddy business of yours."

"If it's no business of ours, then we shall forget it as soon as you've told us."

Bennet laughed. "Not this, you won't." Wearily, he went on, "I guess I'll have to tell you. I went to promise her that from now on I'm right off the ruddy booze. No more ruddy booze for Harry Bennet. That's all! Are you going to forget that in a hurry, you two? I couldn't tell her that with the whole perishing police force listening, could I?"

"I see the point, Bennet. Well, we won't trouble you any more tonight."

The two policemen drove up to Althorp. There were lights in the Bennet house, and Mrs. Bennet did not seem particularly surprised to see her visitors. She was temperamentally hopeful, and the doubtful prospects of her family did not prevent her greeting them with her usual expansive smile.

"We're sorry to trouble you so late at night, Mrs. Bennet."

"No trouble, Inspector, no trouble at all. You saved Mr. Bennet's life, didn't you? I cannot sleep these hot nights, and my little Tommy has teeth coming, and so I am not in bed now."

"We've called to ask for some information. It's possible we may use what you say in evidence. I must warn you of that."

"Anything you say, Inspector. There's nothing to hide here."

Literally, that seemed true enough; the place was very sparsely furnished indeed.

"The first question is: when did you

last see your husband?"

She looked alarmed. "Why, isn't he at the hospital?"

"He was, ten minutes ago. But he broke out earlier, and was away for an hour. I want to know where he went."

She laughed — a jolly laugh. "He came here, of course. But he thought you knew that. He said one of your Punjabis was following him all the way."

"Can you tell me why he came?"

Mrs. Bennet became sober at that, and thought for a moment, evidently trying to make up her mind whether to tell the whole truth or not. Then she said, frankly, "He came to see how I was; he said he was very worried about me. He's a good husband to me, Inspector. I told him he need not worry about me. I'll be all right. I'm used to it, and anyway, it won't be for a week yet."

"That was all?"

She hesitated, and then plunged. "I don't know that I ought to tell you, Inspector, because he said his other reason for breaking out of hospital was to tell me something he didn't want to say in front of the police, and he didn't know when he'd get the chance to say it quite alone. I told him not to be silly, because he'd done nothing wrong, and you can't keep him in jail for drinking himself silly. But he said he wanted to tell me at once what he'd decided. You see, Inspector, my husband is a good man, really, though he does drink too much sometimes. He was sober tonight, and he cried. He made me weep, too. It was so silly. He's lost his job and last night he drank so much he nearly killed himself. And he's sorry now. And what he really came here for was to ask me to forgive him and to promise me he would never drink another drop." Mrs. Bennet put her handkerchief to her eyes, and wiped away the beginnings of tears. "Of course, I forgave him before he asked. He's a good man, really, you see."

"I see," Spearpoint agreed, gravely.

She smiled again. "Of course, he won't keep his promise. I wouldn't hold him to it. A man has to have a bit of fun. But he's had a shock. He ought to be smacked and sent to bed, like one of the kids. But he's too big for me to do that. And, in a way, you've done it for me. So I say to you, Inspector, thank you. Because I know you'll let him come home tomorrow, and then someone will give him a job. Perhaps Mr. Tilson will take him back now Mr. Boreman's out of the way."

"Maybe. Exactly when did your husband go?"

"It was just after Barbara Villiers was set on. We heard a scream, and he said, 'With that row going on in the front, I may be able to slip out the back way without anyone seeing me'. And he just smacked me a kiss and away he went."

"So he was in this room when she screamed?"

"Certain sure he was, Inspector."

It was past eleven when they arrived back at the Police Station. Spearpoint, with Capel at his heels, strode over to the hotel and knocked at the landlord's private door.

"Anderton in?"

"No, sir! Came in about half past six, had dinner, and pushed off about eight without a word. That was the last we've seen of him."

"He said he was going to spend the week-end painting pictures of the bay. Did he?"

"Too right! Sat on the ruddy veranda all yesterday and all this morning, squinting out to sea, and dabbing away at the paper, and then tearing it up and starting again."

"See any of the results?"

"He showed me a couple. Ruddy crude to my mind. Not that I'm a ruddy expert. But when he came back to dinner he tore 'em up, and his whole ruddy week-end's work's gone into the boiler. Best place for it, I reckon."

"Mind if I have a look round his room?"

"As the barmaid said to the bishop, everything we have is at your service."

The room bore the usual signs of occupation, but was tidy. "Look, Capel. I'll smoke a quiet pipe on the veranda;

you go and see if you can find any prints on the knife."

"Can do, sir."

But presently Capel came back to report that the knife was no witness: every smooth surface had been wiped clean. Whoever stabbed Barbara had either worn gloves or else held the knife in a cloth.

"Anderton hasn't come back, and I think I'll turn in. Put a constable on to note when he returns, and to make sure he doesn't go away until we've had a word with him."

Inspector Spearpoint went to sleep almost as soon as his head touched the pillow. He was confident that he had the solution to his problem nicely worked out.

In the morning the constable reported that no one had entered the hotel during the night; and a further visit to Anderton's room confirmed that he had not slept there. Spearpoint deployed all the constables he could lay hands on to search for the missing clerk, and drove up to the hospital with Capel.

Barbara Villiers was sitting up in bed, looking pale, but with her hair neatly combed and a long piece of sticking plaster across her cheek. Her forehead was bruised.

She smiled wanly at the policemen, and received their expressions of condolence and relief with her usual dignified courtesy. All she said was, "I've been worried about the baby; so I told Dr. Fell and he has assured me it's all right, as far as he can tell at this stage. That's all I really care about."

"I'm glad about that, Barbara. But I want to catch whoever it was who tried to kill you. Can you tell us all you remember about the attack?"

"All I can say is that a man sprang on my back out of the bushes as I was entering the garden. He had a knife, and he slashed at my face from behind. I tried to twist round and grab the knife, but he caught me off balance, and he punched me in the side and pushed me over, and

I suppose he stuck the knife in my back. I can't remember it at all clearly. It was all over in a few seconds."

"The fact that he slashed your right cheek suggests that he held the knife in his right hand. Was he directly behind you?"

"Yes. He sort of leapt on my back. He kicked me behind the knee. That's what made me fall, I think. I've got several big bruises." She smiled slightly, and went on, frowning in the effort to recollect. "Let me try again. He jumped on my back, quite suddenly, without any warning. I didn't hear any footsteps. His left hand clutched my left shoulder; he kicked me behind the right knee; I sort of bent forward, and my knee gave. At the same moment he cut my cheek with the knife. I don't know whether he was aiming at my throat and made a bad shot, or whether he wanted to scar my face. I tried to twist round as I was falling, and then I hit the ground with my right knee, and then I suppose I must have banged my head on the concrete. But

I felt the stab in my back. That's all I can remember — except this: a sort of scuffling of his feet on the path. I think perhaps he almost fell over me, and had a job to keep his balance."

"You've certainly remembered remarkably well, considering it all happened in less than half a minute."

"I've been lying here thinking about it."

"You're sure it was a man?"

"That was my impression. It was someone wearing trousers, not a skirt. And leather shoes. It was that kick that made me sure he was a European, and not a barefoot Indian. He wasn't big enough for a native, anyway. Besides, I can't imagine an Indian or a Fijian wanting to murder me — or to slash my face."

"Is it possible that it was a woman in trousers?"

Barbara was doubtful. "I didn't think so, but I suppose it's possible. But I can't think of any woman who'd dress up in order to attack me." She

264

was evidently unconscious of Louise Carwell's enmity — or, at least, of its full intensity.

"I believe you know who it was."

She did not answer that for a moment. Then she agreed, "Yes, I think I do know who he was. But I didn't see him. I couldn't be certain. I couldn't go into the witness-box and swear I recognised him. All I could say was, that he was not a big man, or a very strong one. It's only because I can't imagine anyone else wanting to attack me that I think I know who he was. So I can't tell you, can I?"

Spearpoint tried a bluff. "Suppose I told you that Mr. Anderton's fingermarks were on the knife — would that surprise you at all?"

Her look expressed distaste. "I suppose I may as well admit that that was what I thought."

"What do you think his motive was?"

She hesitated again, and then came out frankly. "I think I'd better tell you about our conversation after we left you yesterday afternoon." She told the story at some length, adding, "You see, I had a sort of instinct about him. In the office, he's always been nice and polite and thoughtful, but I always felt that there was something — well, that he'd turn nasty if he didn't get his own way. I could never have trusted him."

"Yet you trusted Mr. How?"

"That was different. I was in love with Jack. He could do what he liked with me. It was just the way I felt when he was near me. I'm sure I was right about Mr. Anderton, though. — But I couldn't swear in Court that it was him."

"He didn't return to the hotel last night, and I've put search parties on to look for him. If he's alive when we find him, I expect he'll confess to attacking you. You keep safe here and get yourself fit again."

As they drove back to the Police Station, Capel asked, "Could Anderton have done those jobs at the bach?"

"Consider this, Capel: whoever shot

266

Boreman must have fixed up that booby-trap afterwards, pushing the cord under the pillow where the blood-stained head was. That's not the sort of cold-blooded action you'd expect of a nervy chap who screams at the sight of a wounded pigeon. I'm sure that How was killed first; I can't imagine him going off to sleep after the shot had killed Boreman. So whoever killed Boreman must have rifled How's cupboard for the revolver and the ammunition while How was lying dead in the same room. Can you imagine Anderton doing that? To leap on a girl's back and slash at her from behind and push her over and then to run away without waiting to see what damage he's done — that's right up young Anderton's street, though. Still, people are queer, and there's no knowing what a man may do when he's filled himself with whisky and strung himself up to the pitch of rage and desperation."

"I see that, sir; and I can see that a crazy and jealous kid would have slashed at Barbara. I can understand him stifling How from envy. But where did Boreman come in?"

"That's the point, Capel — the key to the problem. The scene was set, very clumsily and hurriedly, to make it seem that How and Boreman killed each other. If How was killed in rage and jealousy, Boreman was killed in cold-blood. I don't say there wasn't hatred there, too; but the prime murder was How's."

Back at the Police Station, Spearpoint was rung by his opposite number in Boscobal.

"Your idea of a search warrant paid off, Spearo. Here's the story. I'll send a written report round as soon as it's typed. As soon as we showed up with the warrant, we could see you were on to something. And we didn't have to look further than Mrs. Boreman's hand-bag. A hundred and sixty-five pounds and some odd silver and copper. All the three marked notes you told me to look for. She said it was her savings she'd brought from Samoa in Fijian notes because she was going to settle down with her husband in Malua. When I asked her why she hadn't declared all the cash to the Customs, she pretended she didn't understand she had to produce more than the minimum to be allowed in. But she couldn't explain how she'd brought from Samoa three notes which were in the bank at Malua when she landed in Suva.

So I brought her down here and charged her with the theft of the notes, and told her she'd been seen in Malua and also that Bulkeley's car had been seen on the Malua road, going out on Saturday evening and coming back on Sunday morning. I've found plenty of evidence there, Spearo.

She decided to play then, and this is her story, believe it or not. She's been living on some family property in Apia, but there's been a law-suit, one of those tangled Samoan ancestral rows, I gather, and she was on the losing end. So she wrote to her husband for money and he told her to go to hell. So she wrote to say she was coming to Malua to sue him for maintenance, and he didn't answer. Mrs. Bulkeley drove her round on Saturday evening, and she walked over to the bach about nine. At the bach, there was a sing-song going on in the room at the end nearest to the entrance to the compound, and she called out to ask if Boreman was there. A man came on to the veranda and told her Boreman was out for the evening. She told him who she was and asked which was her hubby's room, and the man, according to her account, laughed and told her it was the room at the other end of the bach, and advised her to go along and get into bed and wait for Boreman. This man said that Joe Boreman was always talking about his wife, and saying how much he missed her, and how he wished he could come home one night and find her waiting for him in bed, just like the old days. She didn't believe him, and she gave him some Samoan back-chat in reply, and then went away.

Early next morning, she had another

go. It was light, about six o'clock, she says. She went straight along the veranda to the room she'd been told was Boreman's. Everything was quiet, and when she went into Boreman's room, she found him dead in bed. She says he'd been shot through the head; there was a revolver on the floor, and a piece of string tied to the trigger, and altogether a bit of a mess. Of course, it was a ten-sized shock to her; but she's not a particularly sensitive woman, I judge, and I think it's clear that all passion was spent between her and Joe Boreman a dozen years ago. She noticed that one of his legs was stuck up, and the sheet rumpled back, and that he was wearing his day shirt, with a bulging lump in one pocket. She felt the pocket and found it contained a roll of notes. Her story is that she thought it was her husband's money, and that now he was dead, it was hers. So she put the money in her bag. She also cleared a couple of quids' worth of notes and coins out of his pants pocket and looked round the room for any other oddments she thought she was entitled to. She found his keys and looked into his suitcase to see if she could find her letters. She says they weren't there. She won't give any details of what was in 'em, but my guess is that she had been threatening to cut his throat if he didn't ante up. She says she didn't look into any of the other rooms, and that she went straight back to the Bulkeleys'; and as soon as she told Mrs. Bulkeley what she'd seen, they decided to cut back here and lie low and pretend they'd never left Boscobal. Her line is that the money is now hers and she has no idea who shot her husband, so she has no case to answer."

"Nice work, old man. It's what I expected, of course. You'll hold her, won't you?"

"Too true. She's safely in the cooler, meditating on what it feels like to be charged with stealing money out of her own husband's pocket."

As soon as he had rung off, Spearpoint rang the hospital and told them he no longer wanted to hold Harry Bennet; he then gave the same information to Mr. Tilson, who conceded that he would keep the man on.

Half an hour later, a constable who had been sent up towards the hills with a pair of binoculars reported that he had spotted in the far distance along the coast a khaki-clad figure skulking among the mangroves. Within two minutes, Spearpoint and Capel were speeding along the coast road in the police car.

14

Confession Story

THE constable who had picked up the khaki figure from far off had had to leave his observation post to report, and in so doing had lost track of the quarry; but that did not matter since he had no means of communicating with the car speeding along the coast road. All that Spearpoint knew was that the man was some miles to the east and close to the sea.

After traversing Chinese market gardens where blue-dungareed men in cartwheel basket-hats trotted purposefully about their toil, the coast road ran for some miles between canefields, now harvested and burnt off and so desolate. Beyond was irregular ground where a fugitive might have gone to cover. The road here was unkempt, with tufts of rank grass at the edges, and behind them thickets of wild guava and lemon trees, almost choked by parasitic creeper — penetrable bush for anyone who merely wanted to hide within reach of wild fruit. But the man the police sought had been well beyond.

Spearpoint pulled up at a native village which occupied a clearing near a stream which ran down to the sea. Thatched huts were dotted at intervals on the close-cropped grass, and a group of natives were busy building the tree-trunk skeleton of a large *vale ni mothe* (living house). A cheerful crowd gathered round the car and answered Spearpoint's enquiry with evidence that a *turanga* (white man) had indeed walked through the village very early that morning, before anyone was astir. He had been observed, nevertheless, though he had shown no awareness of that. He was hatless, and was wearing khaki shirt and trousers; he had trudged on wearily, looking neither to right nor to left.

A mile further on, they came to the

humble dwelling of an Indian, where a decrepit old man sat outside an even more decrepit corrugated-iron house. Half-a-dozen naked children were playing in the roadway. They shrilled, *"Salaam, sahib!"*as Spearpoint halted; and eagerly assented to his question: a *sahib* had indeed walked that way. It was a marvel: a *sahib* walking; and a very tired and limping *sahib* he was.

How long ago? — Who knows, sahib? An hour; two hours, perhaps.

This was reassuring; for beyond, there was no chance of escape. Capture or suicide was certain. The road ran for miles as close to the shore as a firm causeway could be built. On the left was what passed for the beach — an expanse of flat mud where sticks of mangrove sprouted forlornly. Nowhere there could a man hide. On the right, the whole area was a low-lying swamp, choked with mangroves. Occasionally, on a patch of firm ground, some mango trees struggled for life, wretched little trees with neither the exuberance of youth nor the dignity of age. Creepers clung to their thin trunks and branches, fighting them for what sustenance there was in the soil. They did not wear the creeper with the proud air of having gained adornment; they drooped like old men staggering under unbearable burdens. Only rarely was there a gleam of hope in this desolate land: where a curving palm shot its head clear above the mass, or a clump of ragged-leaved bananas offered food and shade. For the most part, this was a trackless jungle. A man could leave the road only to be stuck in the mud, perhaps to drown. It was Spearpoint's fear that the man he sought would choose such a death, and that his body might never be found.

Two miles beyond the Indian's hut, Spearpoint halted at a chance widening in which he would be able to turn the car.

"It's fourteen hours since Barbara was attacked, and we are fifteen miles away. He can't be far ahead. If he's been walking in this direction all night, he'd be well beyond here by now, but it's clear that he's very tired. He can't be making more than two miles an hour. I think we might lock the car and go on foot for a little way, looking carefully into the bush in case he's hiding."

"What I can't understand is why he ran away."

"Sheer blind animal instinct, I should think. He can't hope to escape. He can't get off the island. He may kill himself before we catch him, of course; but there's no reason why he should wander all this way to do that. I think he's gone beyond reason, though. Which is why he might do anything now."

A few hundred yards on, they caught a glimpse of a khaki garment among the bushes.

He had already seen the two policemen, and as soon as he realised he was observed, he made a frantic effort to hide behind a tree; but he was clinging on with one hand, the branch snapped, and he slipped into the water.

Spearpoint shouted, "You'd better come

out of that, Anderton."

He did not answer. Through the bushes, they could see him floundering, up to his knees in water and slime, trying to pull himself up on branches, and constantly falling back.

They stood and watched him. They were both much heavier men, and they doubted if they could find foothold where he could not; moreover, Spearpoint did not see why they should wade in stinking mud to rescue him if he could eventually rescue himself. The heat was bouncing off the road, and their belt buckles were too hot to touch; a shower-bath would have been delightful, but the marsh was not at all the same thing. Anderton did not make much progress, for though he sometimes got a good grip and hauled himself forward a foot or so, his next effort sucked him back; he was exhausting himself but it did not appear that he was in real danger of drowning.

He made so little progress that presently Spearpoint sent Capel back to the car to fetch a rope from the boot. When Capel returned, Anderton had worked himself into a position where he was clearly visible, but where there was no clear path across which to throw the rope. It was not until the fifth throw that he managed to grasp one end and could be dragged to the firm ground. They made no attempt to ease his passage, and he was scratched and jabbed to screaming point before they had hauled him to hard ground. He arrived on all fours almost in a state of collapse.

Spearpoint asked if he'd had anything to eat or drink lately.

He was sulkily rubbing his scratches and bruises and did not answer for a while, but his self-pity was stronger than his desire to display his resentment, and he panted, "I had some bananas — a couple of hours ago; and a lemon. It was bitter. I'm thirsty."

Capel produced the water-flask he had thoughtfully brought. When he had drained that, Anderton looked a little better. He gazed ruefully at his muddy, blood-smeared legs and his torn shirt; and then he put his hands to his head and sank back on the ground in an attitude of collapse.

Spearpoint felt no sympathy for him. He stirred him rather roughly with his boot. "Come on, get up and we'll take you where you can have a bath and a clean-up."

"I don't want a bath," Anderton muttered. "I want to die."

"That's foolish talk."

"You're going to hang me, aren't you?"

"Not today. I'm going to arrest you for attacking Miss Villiers with intent to inflict grievous bodily harm, but you can't be hanged for that."

Anderton looked up, almost in anguish. "Didn't I kill her, then?" he asked, excited.

"Nowhere near. She's cut and bruised, and her face may be scarred for life, but she'll recover all right."

Anderton uttered a foul oath such as Boreman might have used at the meal-table, and banged his head on the ground in despair. Capel bent and pulled him up, and he struggled, trying to tear himself away.

"Let me go!" he screamed. "I meant to kill her! Let me drown myself! Let me go! I don't want to live!"

Capel held him expertly until the paroxysm passed. Then he marched the wretched youth towards the car. There, Anderton was by turns limp and unresisting, and violently struggling and swearing; so they stripped off his mud-caked clothes and wrapped him in a rug and lashed him up with his arms inside. He was not in any sense insane, but he was acting stupidly, without any self-control, and they had to secure him to make sure he did not do himself — or them — a mischief.

As they drove back to Malua, Anderton had one lucid patch in which he explained himself in an almost normal manner. "I loved that girl, as I told you. I wanted to marry her. I offered to marry her and be a father to Jack How's child, and she turned me down. She'd rather have a nameless bastard than marry me. That was why I decided to kill her and then kill myself. Only somehow I couldn't bring myself to put my head down in the swamp. I did once, but I couldn't keep it down. So I'm just a bloody failure. I didn't kill her, and I couldn't even kill myself." He brooded in silence for a few minutes, and then brightened. "Still, you can hang me for murdering How and Boreman, can't you?"

"You'd better keep your mouth shut," Spearpoint advised him; and whether because he saw the wisdom of that, or because he was utterly weary, he said little for the rest of the ride. But once he burst out, "I wish I'd stayed and finished her off. Then you'd have had to hang me, if you'd caught me with the knife in my hand."

They collected some clean clothes for him from the hotel, and Capel supervised him having a shower and a meal — which restored him to a morose normality. Shortly after one o'clock a clean and fed, but still tired-looking would-be murderer was ushered into the District Inspector's office and sat down in the visitor's chair.

Spearpoint explained that he was under arrest for his attack on Miss Villiers, and cautioned him, adding that if he cared to make a statement Capel would take it down and it might be used in evidence.

"I don't want to be bothered with a solicitor and all that stuff. I'd rather confess and get the whole business over as quickly as possible." He looked across to Capel and signed to him to start writing.

"All I wanted in the world was to marry Barbara Villiers. I saw her when I came over to Malua with the Lautoka cricket team six months ago, and I fell in love with her at sight. I found out that she was the typist at R. L. & Co. and I told Mr. Tilson that I wanted a change from Lautoka and I'd be interested if he ever had a job to offer me. When he wrote and said there was a vacancy in the office, I jumped at it, though it was a pound a month less than Marryan and Cutt were paying me. But when I came here, I found she was in love with Jack How, and he was a hateful fellow. He used to make the most obscene and suggestive remarks about her in the bach. I didn't know what to do, but I thought at first that perhaps I could make her like me. But I didn't make any headway at all. Well, I've told you all this before — what I felt about her, and that she hadn't eyes for anyone but Jack How. And I've told you how I went back to the bach on Saturday night and saw her go into his room. Of course, I didn't know then that she thought she was his wife. I just thought she was a bitch who preferred How to me.

I didn't intend to murder How when I went back to the bach that night, but while I was standing there waiting for her to come out of his room, the idea came to my mind that if I could think of some way whereby it would look as if How and Boreman had killed each other, I might kill How and not be suspected at all. I think it was partly the natives singing and drumming on the beach that stirred me up to murder. I couldn't have dared to kill anyone without all that throbbing in the night.

That drumming did something to me! Ever since that night, something has been going throb — throb — throb in my brain! It's been driving me mad!"

Spearpoint interrupted at that point. "Just a minute! Did you hear them singing *Abide With Me?*"

Anderton was taken aback; he hesitated, flushed, and then muttered, "That was when I was walking home afterwards."

"Did it make any impression on you?"

"I don't know what you mean." But he only said that to gain time. He went on, "No, I can't remember that it did. I heard them singing it in the distance, that's all."

"Go on."

"Where was I?" For a moment he seemed confused; the interruption had put him right off his course. "Oh! well, after she'd gone away, I waited until I thought How would be asleep, and I tiptoed on to the veranda, and he was breathing steadily and snoring a bit; so I crept into his room, and I could see he hadn't bothered to draw the net; and I felt for his rug, and I threw it suddenly over his head, folded thick, and lay with my full weight on top. He thrashed about a bit, but presently he was all still. I kept there and counted three thousand, and then I eased a bit, and he didn't move; so I felt for his heart, and it wasn't beating; so I got off the bed and put the rug back on the trunk. Then I went to his cupboard and took out his revolver and made sure it was loaded, and I took some cord I found in the corner. And I went along to Boreman's room, and he was sleeping all right; so I shot him and fixed up the booby-trap, and then went back to the hotel."

Anderton came to a stop, and Spearpoint asked, "That's all, is it? Just like that?"

"Yes, just like that." Anderton seemed indignant.

"I think you've left a few things out."

Anderton looked worried. "What?"

"You straightened How's limbs?"

Anderton flinched, but recovered and confessed, "Yes, I forgot to mention that."

"You handled a dead body and forgot it?"

"It didn't seem like a dead body. It was still warm — but the horrible thing was, I couldn't believe he was dead, and I thought all the time he'd suddenly put out his arms and grab me by the throat."

"Did Boreman have his knee up when you shot him, or did he raise it in his death agonies?"

"I think it was up all the time. I couldn't bear to try to rearrange him."

"But you could slide your hand under the pillow to put the cord there?"

"I had to do that." Anderton was disintegrating under the questions, and his answers were increasingly incoherent.

"What about the handkerchief?"

After some stammering attempts and

re-starts, Anderton managed to say, "I found it when I picked up the rug; it was lying on top, and I recognised it was hers and it seemed a good idea to use it."

"You thought it might throw a bit of suspicion on her?"

"Well, yes."

"Whereas it only complicated the clear suggestion of mutual murder and helped to spoil your silly little plot."

Anderton resented this. "Well, I only had a few minutes to work out the idea; it wasn't as if I'd been planning it for months."

"Obviously. Did you fire the revolver with your right hand or your left?"

"My right hand, of course."

"Have you ever fired a revolver before?"

Anderton did not know whether to say 'Yes' or 'No' to this. He finally admitted to having fired one once.

"So you were prepared for the kick?"

"Oh, yes."

"Did you use a torch, or did you do it all in the dark?"

"In the dark. I didn't dare show a light."

"You recognised the handkerchief in the dark?"

"I could smell the scent on it."

"That's enough for the time being." But, as the wretched young man was being led away, Spearpoint shot at him one apparently inconsequent question. "You're from Home, aren't you? Did you ever go to the Cup Final?"

The answer came promptly, but with a wondering stare. "Yes, I did once. Why do you ask?"

"Just an idea."

When he had gone, Capel asked, "What was the idea, sir?"

"It was his saying that *Abide With Me* made no impression on him. You know, that tune is something more than just a hymn, to a certain kind of Englishman. It is to me, and I daresay it is to Anderton. I've known quite tough Rugby-playing blokes say that the one thing that makes them want to weep is *Abide With Me*. It's tied up in their memories with childhood, and hearing their mothers singing it, and Sunday School, and with singing it at the Cup Final. Young Anderton is a sentimental Englishman. Think of that tune coming to him across the darkness of the night just after he'd murdered two men in cold blood! It would have shattered him then, and he wouldn't be able to think of that moment now without bursting into tears."

"I get the point, sir. *Abide With Me* always makes me blow my nose. But it's not conclusive is it?"

"Of course not. But you'll remember Barbara said she never went over to the side of the room where the rug was, and he said he found her handkerchief there. That's a detail, too. But I'm sure he's never fired a revolver in his life; and I'm damned sure he couldn't tell if one was loaded or not just by feeling it in the dark."

"He'd have let it off most likely. And I don't see how he could aim at the vital spot in Boreman's head without a light, especially right-handed, screwed up in that corner."

"Yes; and consider this: whoever put that cord under the pillow and tied one end to the bed-post must have leaned right over Boreman, with his face almost touching Boreman's head. A man who'd scream at the sight of a wounded bird couldn't have done that to save his life — neither in the dark knowing the head was there, nor in the light when he could see it. But it isn't only that I don't believe Anderton has the guts to handle a corpse; I don't believe he ever has. Do you remember the first time you handled a dead body? Weren't you impressed by the shocking inertness of it? You pick up a limb and it drops. It's *dead*. He couldn't have straightened How's limbs without having that feeling stamped on his mind. The fact is, Capel, that young man is a bloody liar with the death wish. He no more murdered those two fellows than I did."

15

The Final Story

"NOW, Miss Carwell, we need your help in settling this business, and I can't find out exactly what happened unless you tell me the truth — every bit of it. You haven't told us that yet."

"I have so!"

"You have not! You told us that when Mr. How shone his torch under Mr. Boreman's bed you saw blood dripping on to the floor."

"So I did!"

"You saw blood dripping on to the floor?"

"Yes, I did! A great pool of blood! It was ghastly!"

"There was no blood on the floor next morning."

"I thought I saw blood," she faltered.

"Perhaps it was a shadow in the torch-light."

"And you said you saw a blue silk handkerchief sticking out of the drawer."

"Yes, I did! It belonged to the girl Villiers."

"But the handkerchief was inside the drawer; you could not have seen it from where you say you stood at the door."

"It was hanging over the edge of the drawer when I saw it. It must have slipped in afterwards."

"You said, too, that you heard the natives singing *Isa Lei* a long time after the shot."

"What of it?"

"Several people tell me they heard the shot while the natives were singing *Isa Lei.*"

She burst out angrily, "How can I be expected to be sure about these little details? It was a horrible experience! You can't expect anyone to remember everything exactly in the order in which it happened. Things could have got muddled up in my memory. They would in yours if you'd had to go through what I had to go through!"

As Spearpoint still said nothing, she went on, "People can't remember things exactly. They never can! You want to read some of these murder stories in the books. You'll see there that people remember things in all sorts of order. That doesn't prove that they're liars, or — or killers. It's just that their minds get confused with what they've been through."

"You read a lot of crime stories, don't you?" He asked this in a mild tone, as if he was allowing himself to be side-tracked into a discussion on a subject in which they shared an interest.

"Sometimes. I read a lot — all sorts."

"You've thought about the possibilities of a 'perfect murder', eh?"

She responded eagerly to his academic tone, becoming the expert correcting the tyro. "The story writers say there isn't one. The criminal always makes some silly mistake and gives himself away."

"Like saying he saw something that

wasn't there, but which he thought would be there after he had gone away?"

She reverted to her indignant defensive. "I don't know what you mean!" She knew very well.

"Whoever shot Mr. Boreman might well have thought he would go on bleeding and that the blood would soak through the bedding and drip on to the floor. But corpses don't bleed much and there was very little blood even in the bed. Whoever shot Mr. Boreman might have left the handkerchief conspicuously on the edge of the drawer, and would not know it had been insecurely balanced and had slipped into the drawer a minute or two afterwards."

"It was balanced on the drawer when I saw it. That was only a few minutes after the shot, you know."

"How do you know the handkerchief belonged to Miss Villiers? You only saw it in the torchlight across the room for a few seconds."

"Because she had one that colour and she had been in the bach, and she'd been crying, I thought it was hers."

Spearpoint changed the subject abruptly. "You're left-handed, aren't you?"

"No, I'm not. Why do you ask?"

"Whoever shot Mr. Boreman must have been left-handed — "

"But I didn't shoot him anyway!"

" — because there wasn't room between the head of the bed and the wall and the chest-of-drawers for anyone to stand and fire right-handed at the angle that the bullet went through his head."

She pondered that for a moment, suspecting a trap, or perhaps wondering how silly a Police Inspector could be. "I don't know about that," she plunged. "Couldn't a man as slender as Mr. How have stood with his back to the wall and fired across his front right-handed?"

"Show me how you mean."

She sprang to her feet, eager to teach these stupid policemen their business, and went over to the wall by a filing cabinet and took stand with her back to the wall and her right hand across her front, crouching slightly to about the height from which the bullet had gone.

"But," Spearpoint objected, "he couldn't have aimed so neatly without a light. Could he have aimed straight, crouching like that and holding his torch in his left hand?"

"I don't see why not."

"But if he'd gone into the room and switched on his torch, Mr. Boreman might have woken up while he was getting into that complicated position to fire."

"He could have got into position first. It wasn't all that dark. And if he switched on the torch and fired at once, Boreman wouldn't have had time to wake up."

"He certainly didn't wake up." Spearpoint addressed Capel meditatively. "Yes, I suppose that's how she did it."

Louise strode to his desk, storming at him. "I did not do it! It was Jack How who shot him!"

"I did not say it was you. I said it was a woman. It could not have been Mr. How. He must have been dead by then. He would never have fallen asleep with a corpse in the bungalow. Besides, a woman was seen to leave the bach ten minutes after the shot was fired."

"That was the girl Villiers! I saw her!"

Louise glared at Spearpoint across the desk and he met her gaze steadily. Few people ever out-stared him, and Louise was not to be one of them.

She turned away and sat down with a defiant twirl of her skirts. "If it had been me, there would have been my fingerprints on Mr. How's torch."

"His torch had a serrated surface which doesn't take fingerprints."

The buzzing of the intercom broke the tension.

"Yes? — All right, ask her to wait a minute. — I'm sorry, Miss Carwell, I must interrupt this interview for a few minutes. The witness who can give me the last piece of evidence and tell me who that woman was has just come in. I must ask you to wait outside for a few minutes."

"I don't see why I should stay here

any longer. I've told you all I know. You can't prove I killed them."

"I'm asking you to wait because I need your help to clear this business up."

"Well, Katarina, I hope you caught plenty of fish."

The Fijian girl intimated with a shy giggle that the expedition had been a successful one.

"Good! Well, now you've come ashore and we've found you, I have to ask you some very serious questions. Don't be afraid to tell us the truth, because I'm not blaming you for anything; it's other people we want to know about. If you can tell us anything important, I may have to get you to give evidence in Court. You understand what that means, don't you; and that you must tell the truth?"

"I understand. I will tell you the truth."

"Were you at the Bulkeleys' house all Saturday night?"

"*Eo, saka.*" ('Yes, sir.')

"Was Mrs. Bulkeley there?"

"Eo, saka."

"Was there anyone with her?"

Katarina hesitated, but when Spearpoint told her that he knew that Mrs. Boreman had been in Malua on Saturday night, she became communicative and gave him an evidently truthful glimpse into the big woman's visit to the West Coast.

The two ladies had arrived by car about eight o'clock, and, after a snack, Mrs. Boreman had gone out for a stroll; she had returned after about an hour, and the two ladies had sat up until nearly two o'clock, dressmaking. Katarina had stayed up too, partly to prepare and clear away a midnight three-course meal, and partly to serve as model for the dress Mrs. Boreman was cutting down as a present for her. She had thought that the sole purpose of the overnight visit to Malua had been to make use of Mrs. Bulkeley's sewing-machine to work up some material Mrs. Boreman had brought from Samoa as a present for Mrs. Bulkeley. She had heard neither of the ladies mention Mrs. Boreman's husband.

301

Katarina, who slept in a hut in the garden, had been roused early on Sunday morning — she did not know the time, but hazarded the guess that it had been around eight — and told that the ladies were going back to Suva at once, and that she could have a holiday for the rest of the week. So she had gone fishing with her brothers.

"Did they ask you not to tell anyone they had been to Malua?"

"Mrs. Bulkeley did not say anything about that; but Mrs. Boreman gave me five shillings, and told me not to tell anyone she had been in Malua. I have not told my brothers, but I know I must tell the Inspector, even if I have to give back the five shillings."

"That's a good girl, Katarina. I don't think Mrs. Boreman will expect you to give back the five shillings."

When Katarina had gone, Sergeant Jonitani Tamata came in with a report from the *turanga ni koro* of Mataveithengge, written in the beautiful copperplate of the *Kaiviti* who takes pride in his penmanship. The vital passage was:

"When midnight brought Sunday, we sang Christmas carols, and the typewriter *marama* came and sat to listen to our singing. We offered her *yanggona,* and she drank, and we sang *Isa Lei,* and she sang *Isa Lei* with us; and then she went home, and we sang *Abide With Me* to accompany her up the hill."

"Now, Miss Carwell: a woman was seen to leave the bach ten minutes after the shot was fired; but the man who saw her was too far away to recognise who she was."

"I saw her, too. It was the girl Villiers!"

"It could not have been Miss Villiers. She was on the beach, singing *Isa Lei* with the natives when the shot was fired. And after that she went up the hill to Althorp in the opposite direction to the bach."

Louise said nothing, but she kept glancing round the room like a hunted animal.

"Do you still maintain that Mr. How

went calmly off to sleep knowing there was a dead man in the bach? Why didn't he send you for the police while he waited by the body?"

"Because he'd shot him himself, see!"

"He shot Mr. Boreman and then went to bed?"

Louise became argumentative. Her voice rose as she insisted on making her point. "I never said he went to bed, clever! I don't know what he did after I left him. But he'd been drinking, you know. His breath smelt awful. He seemed drowsy. Perhaps he felt sleepy and lay down for a moment and went off to sleep."

"But he didn't just lie down; he got comfortably into bed."

Louise saw her chance and dug her point home savagely. "He didn't pull out the mosquito net, did he?"

"No, that's true," Spearpoint conceded, as if puzzled. Louise lunged with all her force. "And he didn't take his shoes off, did he?"

"That's true, he didn't," Spearpoint

agreed. *"How do you know?"*

She was not so quick to see she had left her guard wide open. She mumbled vaguely that someone must have told her.

"Who could have told you? Apart from Dr. Fell, Mr. Capel and I, the only person who knew he was found with his shoes on was the murderer who straightened out his limbs and pulled the sheet over him. And the only other people who knew the net wasn't pulled out were two men you have not met since they saw the body."

She sat with her head down, biting her lips savagely. "Some of your story was true. You certainly hid under the bach and overheard the conversations in Mr. How's room; but all that stuff about his kissing you and showing you Mr. Boreman's body was a pack of lies."

"It was not! It was all true!"

"I don't believe you. I believe you murdered them both. I'll tell you what happened. You try to prove me wrong. Until Saturday night you were in love with Mr. How. He took you to the pictures a few times and you built up a whole fantastic dream-world on the idea that he would marry you. And you still thought that when he took up with another girl. But when you overheard that conversation on Saturday night you realised that he felt nothing but contempt for you and that he had in fact married your rival. And from that moment your love turned to hate." He turned to Capel. "Someone was quoting a line of poetry to me the other day. How does it go?"

"You mean Congreve, sir? 'Heaven has no rage like love to hatred turned, Or hell a fury like a woman scorned'? We did it at school." He paused. "The play, I mean."

"That's it. That was you, Miss Carwell. You lay out in the compound planning how to kill Mr. How and fasten the blame on someone else. You hated Mr. Boreman for the vile thing he had said about you; so you planned a mutual murder. As soon as you heard Mr. How snoring you crept into his room and smothered him with his rug, and arranged his body under the sheet. In looking for his revolver you came across Miss Villiers' handkerchief and decided to use that to incriminate her as well. You shot Mr. Boreman, rigged up the booby-trap — which didn't deceive the police for a moment — and then went home. That was the truth of what happened, isn't it?"

There was no answer, but Spearpoint knew that he was staring into the eyes of a murderer desperately at bay.

On being formally charged with the two murders and asked whether a solicitor or anyone else should be invited to the police station, the murderer suddenly found voice.

"Of course I killed them! They hated me, and I hated them! They thought I wasn't fit to associate with them. So I showed them! You think you're clever because you think you've caught me out, don't you? But you're not going to hang me!"

With a sudden twist, the screaming

murderer eluded Capel's grasp and leapt head foremost at the large window behind the desk. It was a brave, effective and bloody suicide.

THE END

A GENTEEL LITTLE MURDER
Philip Daniels

Gilbert had a long-cherished plan to murder his wife. When the polished Edward entered the scene Gilbert's attitude was suddenly changed.

DEATH AT THE WEDDING
Madelaine Duke

Dr. Norah North's search for a killer takes her from a wedding to a private hospital.

MURDER FIRST CLASS
Ron Ellis

Will Detective Chief Inspector Glass find the Post Office robbers before the Executioner gets to them?

STAB IN THE BACK
Malcolm Gray

During a country weekend, a brash young comedian is stabbed to death. Detective Inspector Neil Lambert has to decide who hated the comic enough to ring down the curtain . . . forever.

FRED IN SITU
Gerald Hammond

As a bored hospital patient, Beau Pepys begins to wonder about a night watchman who had disappeared. What starts as a mental exercise gradually raises questions as to what happened to Fred, why and where.

OUT OF THE PAST
Margaret Carr

Steve had killed a man. He was dangerous Angela was told. But she ignored the warnings. She didn't imagine that there might be more than one kind of danger in standing by her old friend.